Neighbours™ 8

It was a ghastly predicament to be in; Helen Daniels was being torn apart by it. It was completely wrong, completely immoral. She was in love.

But it wasn't just the fact that she was in love, certainly no uncommon thing for a woman of her age, mother and grandmother of grownup children; the problem was that she was in love with the man her daughter intended to marry. And to make it worse, the man Rosemary intended to marry was in love with her. And Rosemary suspected nothing. It was an awful mess.

NEIGHBOURS™ 8

Carl Ruhen

From an original concept by Dave Worthington, Ysabelle Dean, Greg Millin, John Linton, Ray Kolle, David Phillips, Jeffrey Truman, Reg Watson, Ginny Loundes, Penny Fraser, Chris Schofield, Geoff Newton, Rick Maier, Betty Quin, John Upton, Ray Harding, Marie Trevor, Ian Smith, Chris McCourt, Cheredith Mok, Wayne Doyle, Lois Booton, Maureen Ann Moran

S T A R

Published by
the Paperback Division of
W.H. Allen & Co Plc

A Star Book
Published in 1989
by the Paperback Division of
W.H. Allen & Co Plc
Sekforde House, 175–9 St John Street, London EC1V 4LL

Neighbours™ © 1989 Grundy Television Pty Ltd
Novelisation copyright © Horwitz Grahame Pty Ltd 1989

Phototypeset by Input Typesetting Ltd, London
Printed and bound in Great Britain by
Cox & Wyman Ltd, Reading

ISBN 0 352 324244

One

'Scoop,' Charlene said after a moment's consideration. 'Scoop Robinson. That's what we'll have to call you from now on.'

'Cut it out.' Scott gave an embarrassed but nevertheless pleased smile. Scoop Robinson? Of course, she was only teasing him. 'I've only sold one article—so don't get carried away.'

'That article got you two hundred and fifty bucks,' Charlene reminded him.

Two hundred and fifty bucks: three weekly instalments, beginning on Saturday. As if he needed reminding of the fact that the local Erinsborough newspaper had paid him two hundred and fifty bucks for the article he had written about his grandmother, Bess Robinson, intrepid traveller and chronicler of the world's more distant and inaccessible peoples and places—something she had encouraged him to do before she set out on that last journey, knowing that this time she wouldn't return. He was on his way; a career had been launched.

'I'd better get mobile,' he said. There were stories out there just waiting to be broken, in-depth and hard-hitting interviews to be conducted, frauds and scandals to be revealed to a deserving public, deadlines to be met, by-lines and commendations in the offing. Scoop? He mulled over the word. Why not? It might sound a bit corny, but . . . why not? He kissed Charlene. 'I'd better get this cheque into the bank,' he said.

'Sure,' she called after him. 'And put a deposit on the Ferrari while you're there.'

5

'That's cute.' He pulled a face. 'Cute. Very cute.'

His name was in print—not very large print, it was true, but right there on page seven of the *Erinsborough News*, under the headline 'Parasols and Poisoned Darts—Bess Robinson—Explorer Extraordinary'. He pointed triumphantly to his name in smaller print beneath the headline. 'This is just the start,' he promised. 'You'll have to get used to seeing that name in print.'

He had just burst into the Robinson kitchen that Saturday morning with an armful of papers, tossing copies down in front of his father, grandmother and little sister, who had said in an awed voice, 'Gee, Scott, this means you're really famous now.'

Helen Daniels was studying her grandson's article. 'It's come up very well,' she observed.

Scott preened. 'Thanks.'

Jim Robinson smiled up at his son. 'Congratulations, mate. Bess would have been very proud of you.'

Hardly a word in the article had been changed, Scott had been overjoyed to discover. There were photographs of Bess, on a camel, in a canoe and halfway along the Hindu Kush. 'She would indeed,' Helen agreed.

Jim had become serious again. 'I hope this convinces you of the need to go back to school again and get your grades,' he said. 'You'll need them if you intend to become a full-time journalist.'

Scott was determined not to let his swelling pride be deflated by sober words from his father who never missed an opportunity to show that he had his feet planted well and truly on the ground. He waved aside his father's advice. 'Who needs school?' he queried loftily. 'I'm already on my way.'

And on his way he was. Ideas were already seething and bubbling inside his creative head. There were stories out there—the world was full of them—and what better place on which to concentrate at the outset—to get his hand in, so to speak—than his own street, charged as it was with drama and human passions although perhaps not on a scale that could properly be described as majestic, or titanic, or the stuff of which Greek tragedy was made, but full of human interest nevertheless? Character sketches, quirks and foibles—Ramsay Street had them in plenty. All he would need to do was change a few names, perhaps embellish a little here and there . . . It wouldn't be too difficult, a piece of cake, in fact. He would write a series of articles that would make him a household name in the district, never mind what his father said about going back to school to obtain the grades which had already hopelessly eluded him.

But his father was still trying to bring him back down to earth. 'Just because they published the article you wrote about my mother,' he said, 'it doesn't mean that they will publish every one you submit. You still have a lot to learn about journalism.'

'Experience,' Scott fervently pointed out to him. 'That's the only way to learn. Get out there—out and about. Talk to people, sniff out the facts. The more I write, the better I'll become. It's just a matter of hard slog. Don't you worry, Dad,' he added, a touch patronisingly. 'Before you know it, everyone will be talking about me.'

As he had thought, it was a piece of cake; the words just seemed to flow out of him. He typed vigorously and made a lot of typing errors. He showed the finished product to Charlene. 'Pretty terrific, eh?' he said with a complacent smile as she read with a deepening frown.

'Are you kidding?' She looked up at him. 'If this gets published, it will cause such a stink that you'll never hear the end of it.'

Scott's smile faded. 'What's wrong with it?'

'All hell's going to break loose, that's what's wrong with it.'

'That's the purpose of it,' Scott said defensively. 'These articles I'm writing are going to make me a household name.'

'They sure will,' Charlene remarked drily. 'And I wouldn't like to be called it.'

Scott was hurt and puzzled by her reaction; he had

7

expected something more positive and reassuring. 'But tell me, what's wrong with it?'

'You'll hurt people,' Charlene replied as she dropped the typescript onto the table.

'I haven't used their real names,' Scott protested.

'You've used everything else.'

'So? Nobody's going to guess.' Picking up the typescript, he rose to his feet, a deeply wounded young man. 'I thought at least you would understand.'

'Scott, I do.' She looked back at him levelly. 'But this is no way to impress your father.'

'What do you mean?' Scott was taken aback by this unexpected statement.

'Well, that's what you're trying to do, isn't it?' Charlene returned. 'Prove he's wrong. Show him you can make it as a journalist.' She gestured towards the typescript in his hand. 'And that's not the way to do it.'

'It's not just that.' Scott was on the defensive again. 'My exam results were like a kick in the stomach—you know that. I mean, you guys all did so well . . .'

'You didn't do so . . .'

'And then the *Erinsborough News* published the Bess Robinson story,' Scott went on with increasing fervour. 'Suddenly, I feel as if I'm worth something . . . that I've found something I can do . . . and I'm not going to let that go, no matter what.'

He was moving to the door when she stopped him. 'I'm sorry, Scott,' she said softly.

'I just wanted you to give me a hand, that's all.'

'With your writing?'

Scott nodded glumly. 'Doesn't seem to be much point now.'

Charlene smiled. 'All right then,' she said. 'Maybe we should go back to your place and get that thing typed up again. There are an awful lot of spelling mistakes for one thing.'

'Never my strong point.' Scott smiled ruefully back at her. 'I thought you didn't approve.'

'Maybe I don't exactly.' Charlene took his hand. 'But far

be it from me to stifle the creative genius,' she said as she led him towards the door.

The following Saturday's edition of the *Erinsborough News* contained a Scott Robinson double. There was the second instalment of the Bess Robinson adventures, and a new feature, which, under the heading 'Diary of a Teenager,' purported to be a fictional account of the activities of a certain group of people in a certain street of a certain suburb that bore characteristics not unlike those of the district in which the *Erinsborough News* was circulated. Once again, excited and anxious that his friends and relatives should share in his achievement, Scott was up and about bright and early to collect copies of the paper that carried both his stories. The last thing on his mind was that the reaction could be anything other than favourable.

Mike Young and Jane Harris were just opening up Daphne Clarke's coffee shop for the day's business when Scott burst in on them with his newspapers. 'Hi there, guys,' he greeted them with a broad grin, then held up one of the papers. 'Have you seen this?'

They regarded him stonily. 'Yeah,' Mike said without enthusiasm.

Not fazed by his tone, or yet aware that anything might be wrong, Scott laughed happily. 'Then how about it? Two stories in the one issue. Have you guys read them both?'

'No,' Mike replied coldly. 'Just the one about Des and Daph.'

Des and Daph? Ah yes, well, as a source—definitely as a source, as background, but building up from there, adding a few things here and there. Human interest, a little spice. He had actually chuckled a few times as he was writing this story about an accountant called Les whose wife, Daisy, was an ex-stripper who ran a boutique. No sweat there; no one would twig to the fact that he was actually writing about a bank manager called Des and his wife, Daphne, who, although she had once earned her living as a stripper, was in fact the proprietor of the coffee shop in the Lassiter Hotel complex. 'Well, it's . . . it's not Des and Daphne exactly,' he hedged in the face of the hostility

9

Mike and Jane were showing him. 'I jazzed it up a bit, that's all, made it more interesting.'

Mike was glaring at him. 'You just don't care, do you?' he cried angrily.

'Eh?' Scott was taken aback by the vehemence of his tone.

Mike was advancing on him threateningly. 'You and your stupid stories.'

'Hey, hang on . . .' Just because Mike lived with Des and Daphne, that didn't mean he had to take it so personally. 'Just listen for a minute . . .'

But Mike was obviously not prepared to listen. 'You don't care who you hurt with your stupid stories,' he shouted as he lunged forward and knocked the papers out of Scott's hands.

The papers were scattered across the floor of the coffee shop. With a groan, and perplexed by Mike's outburst, Scott dropped to his hands and knees to gather them together. 'Good one, mate,' he muttered.

Jane had moved between them. She looked reproachfully at Mike. 'I thought you would have realised by now that aggro doesn't solve anything.'

'Well, I'm sorry,' Mike murmured uncomfortably. 'I lost my temper.'

'I noticed,' Scott said drily from the floor. 'Look,' he went on earnestly, 'I didn't mean to upset anyone. It was only meant to be a fun article.'

'Des and Daphne don't think it's much fun.'

Oh, so they had seen it already. Scott had been sure they would see the humorous side to it. 'How many people are going to know it's them?' he queried. 'Only the people who already know about them.'

Jane studied him gloomily. 'I'm afraid Nan's probably on the phone right now, making sure everyone knows it was the Clarkes you were writing about.' Scott stared at her. Jane's Nan? Jane's grandmother? Mrs Mangel on the phone? Oh God, she would have been onto it like a shot; she wouldn't have wasted a single moment. 'I don't know why you did it,' Jane said sadly.

Scott still battled to defend his actions. 'You can write best about what you know best,' he said. 'That's what Bess—my grandmother—told me. She told me to base my characters on the people I know.'

Jane was clearly unimpressed by this argument. 'I still think you were asking for trouble,' she said.

'So do I,' Mike said with a nod. 'All that stuff about Des having an affair . . .'

'It's not true, Mike,' Scott protested, 'so why should it worry anyone?' Of course Des wasn't having an affair; he and Daphne were a happily married couple. It was just something extra Scott had added to his story about the ex-stripper and her accountant husband. A little spice; poetic licence, if you like. What was it he had written? Something to do with the fact that Des—Les, the accountant—had been engaged so many times that he was finding it difficult to settle down with just the one woman, and already his eye had begun to roam. No harm in that, surely.

'But how are people to know what *is* true in your story,' Jane demanded, 'and what isn't?' She shook her head in disappointment. 'I think you've been pretty thoughtless.'

'*Thoughtless?*' Scott started as a voice vibrant with outrage filled the room from the open doorway behind him. 'Thoughtless?' Daphne repeated as he swung to face her and saw to his dismay the undisguised hatred in her eyes and in the fierce set of her mouth. 'That's not what *I* would call it. I'd call it selfish, cruel . . .' A muscle twitched at the corner of her mouth; she gestured furiously . . . 'absolute lies.'

Clutching the papers to his chest, Scott was on his feet again. 'Aw, listen, Daph . . .'

'Don't "listen" *me*, Scott.' She pointed a quivering and accusing finger at him. 'You've humiliated me—and you've put Des in a very embarrassing position. And I'd like you out of my shop—now.'

Scott still tried to placate her. 'Don't you think you're over-reacting . . . ?'

'I said, out.' Now Daphne's finger was pointing to the

door, as she fixed him with an expression of pure menace. 'Now!'

Seeing that she was not in a mood to listen to anything he might have to say to her, seeing that she was so completely riled up about the matter, Scott shrugged helplessly and backed to the door.

'Okay,' he said. 'I'll talk to you about it later . . .'

'*Out!*'

His bafflement at Daphne's unexpected behaviour remained with him all the way home. He just couldn't understand why she should have carried on in that way. It wasn't as if he had deliberately set out to hurt her and Des. A little harmless fun, that was all it had been. Suddenly, he felt quite deflated; the reactions he had encountered so far were totally different from what he had anticipated. Nor was there any improvement when he did reach home and found his father waiting for him with a stern expression on his face.

'I want to have a word with you,' Jim Robinson said, emerging from the dining room as Scott, carrying his copies of the *Erinsborough News* entered the kitchen by the back door.

'Oh?' With a sense of foreboding, Scott put his papers down on the kitchen table.

'Des and Daphne came by.'

'Oh.' Realising he was about to come in for some more unfair criticism, Scott tried to casually shrug it off. 'Yeah, I've seen Daph.' With a rueful smile, he shook his head. 'Talk about over-react . . .'

'What did you expect?' Jim demanded.

'It wasn't as if I *named* them,' Scott returned defensively. 'Look,' he went on with the heavy sigh of a man greatly misunderstood, 'anyone would think I was being really vicious or something. It was only a piece of satire. I mean, I took a real-life situation and pushed it just that little bit further to get the humour out of it. And what could be wrong with that? All great writers did that, didn't they?'

'Oh yes, there was humour all right,' Jim conceded.

Scott's spirits immediately rose. 'You liked it, didn't you, Dad?' he asked hopefully. 'The way it was written?'

'Yes, well . . . ,' Jim nodded slowly and gave the faintest shadow of a smile. 'Yes, I have to admit that there was the odd chuckle or two.' He became stern again. 'But they were at the expense of people we know, Scott—and that wasn't a smart thing to do. We're a close-knit community here in Erinsborough—here in Ramsay Street in particular.' He shook his head in reproach. 'You're supposed to be creating fiction, not friction.'

Of course his father was taking it too seriously, just as Daphne had taken it too seriously. 'They'll get over it, Dad. It's only because Mrs Mangel has been stirring things up. Look, I'll go and apologise to Des—okay? And I'll bet you that he is not going off his head the way Daphne is.'

'I wouldn't bet on that at all if I were you,' Jim said glumly. 'Des is the one who is talking about libel suits.'

Scott suddenly felt a little weak. He recalled the assurance that the editor of the *Erinsborough News* had given him when the subject of libel was briefly raised. 'Mister Cutler said it wasn't libellous.'

'Probably not,' Jim said. 'And probably Des won't take it that far. But if I were you, I would keep right out of his way for the time being. I mean, the implication that Des was having some sort of an affair was most unfortunate.'

'But, Dad,' Scott protested, 'that was only to add a bit of spice. The article needed brightening up a bit. Des and Daph seemed kind of dull without it.'

Jim compressed his lips. 'They probably *prefer* to be thought dull than to be the subject of local gossip,' he remarked.

Scott was still bemused by these reactions to an exercise that, to him, had been a lark more than anything else. 'I just can't *believe* how everybody is being so small-minded about this,' he said in a wondering tone. 'I mean, an author has the right to draw on real life as an inspiration.'

Jim regarded him bleakly. 'Now don't get carried away with this *author* bit, mate,' he said. 'You're not Hemingway. You're not Fitzgerald or MacBean. What you have to realise is that you have caused people distress—and you have no right to do that, for whatever reason.'

'I still think they're being too touchy,' Scott said with a last attempt at defiance. 'Daphne was really cut up about it.'

'Well, she's pregnant,' Jim observed at the precise moment when, in the house next door, Daphne herself, having briefly anguished over the rights and wrongs of it, had made up her mind to steam open the pink, faintly perfumed envelope addressed to her husband, that had arrived in that morning's post. 'Women get emotional at times like that.'

When Mrs Mangel, a towering pillar of outrage, transferred her account from his bank, it was just one incident in a stressful day for Des Clarke. He was hardly prepared, on his arrival home, to be confronted with any accusations prompted by the letter Daphne had steamed open, read, and re-read, first with incredulity then mounting anger, resealed, then with difficulty tried to pretend idle curiosity about it to Des, been quite persistent about it, then given the game away by wondering why, if it was a business letter, as Des claimed, *she*, meaning the writer of the letter, hadn't sent it to the bank. She? Des rounded on her. Had Daphne been reading his private correspondence? Daphne had to confess that she had read the letter from Des's former fiancée in Tasmania. The atmosphere became quite heated; insults and sarcastic remarks were exchanged. Des stormed angrily out of the house.

The whole thing seemed to be getting out of hand. Des moved in with Clive Gibbons, and Eileen Clarke, distressed about what had happened and muttering about the evils of yellow journalism, moved in with Daphne. In the meantime, Scott was working on the second article in his series, 'Diary of a Teenager'. He wasn't finding this one so easy as the last; the floor around him was littered with screwed up sheets of paper he had pulled out of his typewriter in disgust; he was becoming increasingly frustrated.

'If that's another chapter of your so-called diary,' Jim Robinson said as he gently putted another golf ball across the carpet, 'I hope you'll be more careful this time. I don't want any more neighbours knocking our door down.'

'Aw, come on, Dad,' Scott said peevishly. 'It's all right. Nothing's going to happen.'

'So who's the next victim?' Jim asked. 'It's not us, is it?'

'Of course not,' Scott said uneasily.

Jim putted another ball. 'Then I suppose we should be grateful for small mercies, ' he observed wrily.

Not wishing to be questioned any further about his intentions, Scott stood up and moved away from his father's desk where he had been typing. 'I'll be in my room,' he muttered.

'No, hold it,' Jim said said sharply, and pointed to the chair his son had just vacated. 'Sit down.' Scott sat down. 'Who is it?' Jim demanded.

Seeing that he had no choice but to tell him, Scott said in a small voice, 'The Mitchells, and Mrs Mangel.'

Jim smiled grimly. 'Got something nice and punchy for them, have you?'

Scott was immediately on the defensive again. 'Look, Dad,' he said slowly and emphatically, 'the articles are called 'Diary of a Teenager'. The editor said they don't have to be all that accurate, because it's . . . they're written from my own point of view. It's called subjective licence.'

Leaning on his putter, Jim laughed shortly. 'More like a licence to kill the truth, if you ask me.'

Scott glared resentfully up at his father. 'You're trying to ruin my big chance,' he muttered.

'You know me better than that.' Jim shook his head. 'I'm talking facts, Scott,' he went on after a brief pause during which he shrewdly regarded his son, the aspiring journalist. 'Not rumours, not lies—but facts. Facts your editor is obviously not too concerned about. First, despite what he says, I think there's still a good chance that we could end up with a handful of law suits over these articles; and second, and more importantly, there is your integrity as a writer to consider.' Scott sat stiffly on the chair and listened to his father as he continued. 'You see, Scott, journalism isn't worth a damn without integrity. Some-

15

times, when a country goes wrong, when a government decides to throw all laws and principles out the window, the only truth left comes from the press. Journalists have been murdered for defending that right. Telling the truth is a decision a reporter, a journalist makes every day of his working life. You see, the awful responsibility is that people *believe* what you write—and you're taking advantage of all that integrity at the expense of your neighbours.'

It had been quite a speech from his father, usually a man of few words, and Scott was quite shaken by it. His father had spoken softly, and earnestly, and his words had had an uncomfortable ring of truth to them. Scott was suddenly very worried.

That evening, when Eileen Clarke stormed into the house and demanded to see Scott, he was horrified to learn that Des and Daphne had separated, and that it had been his fault, a direct result of his rumour-mongering article in the *Erinsborough News*. She called him a home-wrecker who deserved to be punished, and if it had been up to her alone she would have sued him on the spot. He could imagine how Daphne must have felt when, just after reading about Des's extra-marital fling, she had found the letter from his former fiancée in Tasmania. He had no right to go round hurting people the way he had.

'I made it up, Dad,' Scott protested after Jim and Helen had finally and thankfully eased the irate woman out of the house. 'Honestly. I didn't know it was true.'

Helen regarded him severely. 'You don't learn at all, do you, Scott?' she said. 'Nobody is saying that what you wrote *is* true—except Daphne. And that's only because she believes your story.'

Scott was feeling utterly miserable. How was he to know that something like this would happen? An awful coincidence. 'Please, Gran,' he murmured, 'I feel bad enough as it is.'

'What are you going to do about it?' Jim demanded.

Scott knew he was referring to the other story he had delivered to the newspapers. 'They don't start printing until midnight,' he said bleakly. 'Maybe I could stop the story,

16

and then . . . then go to Daphne and explain the whole thing.'

'That's the shot.' Jim smiled briefly. 'Do you want me to come with you?'

'No, Dad.' No, he would handle this alone; it was a mess which he got into alone. 'If I'm going to cop it from everyone,' he said dejectedly, 'I might as well cop it by myself.'

But by the time he returned from the newspaper office where the editor had been at pains to assure him that if he pulled out every piece from the paper that upset someone only the advertisements would be left, Scott had changed his mind. There were two sides, he said, to every story. 'It's my career, Dad. And you shouldn't censor the press.'

Jim was clearly annoyed by his son's turnabout. 'Not when the press prints facts,' he said tightly. 'But you're not dealing with facts pure and simple. You're mixing up lies and rumours to exploit friends and neighbours.'

But Scott's mind was made up; he was sticking to his ground. 'It's my decision, Dad,' he said with finality. 'I'm standing by what I wrote.'

Jim was just managing to check his temper. 'How could you . . . ?'

'Just a minute, Jim.' Helen stepped forward. 'Let's just try to see this from Scott's point of view,' she suggested.

'What?' Jim gave her a startled look.

'Just thinking ahead,' Helen said quietly, then turned to her grandson. 'I suppose the second article is as spicy as the first?'

Scott shifted uncomfortably. 'Mister Cutler liked it, yes . . .'

'And the Mitchells are in it?'

'Yes . . .'

'You see?' Helen smiled at Jim. 'You have to admire the boy's convictions,' she said. 'He's obviously prepared to sacrifice everything for his profession.'

For a moment, Scott didn't realise what she was getting at—and then, with sickening force, it came to him. Oh God . . . 'Charlene,' he breathed. What had he gone and done? Mavis Matthews and her beautiful daughter Charlotte . . . The thought of what Madge Mitchell's reaction would be when she read, among other things, about how her alter ego's husband had run off with another woman, and how her son Horace had been gaoled for stealing, suddenly, for the first time, chilled him to the marrow.

Even when he rose very early the following morning to collect the papers which had been delivered to the house in the street—an extremely furtive operation carried out in the half-light of dawn—he knew that there was no real hope that Madge's attention wouldn't be drawn to the article sooner or later.

'Well, hello Scott,' Madge Mitchell greeted him with a manner that was much too friendly for it not to be assumed. 'You're nice and early.'

'Oh, Mrs Mitchell.' With a sinking sensation, Scott guessed she had already seen the article, or at least heard about it. 'I was wondering . . .'

'Of course you were, Scott,' Madge said with devastating sweetness. 'And I've been wondering, too.' The broad, obviously forced smile vanished, to be replaced by a coldly implacable expression. 'I've been wondering why you bother to call me Mrs Mitchell. What happened to . . . what was it? Oh yes, Matthews? Mavis Matthews, Mavis the barmaid whose husband left her for a younger woman who could offer him more fun in life.'

'Ah . . .' Scott began to stammer. 'I . . . I see you've already read it.'

'Read it?' Madge snapped back at him. 'I've already had half of Erinsborough knocking on the door to tell me how famous I am. I didn't have to read it. They read it for me.'

'I changed the names,' Scott said feebly. 'How could they . . . ?'

'*How*?' Madge laughed unpleasantly. 'Mavis for Madge? Charlotte for Charlene? Horace and Frank for Henry and Fred? Honestly, I don't know why you bothered.'

'Yeah . . . well,' Scott muttered awkwardly. 'I can see that now . . . and, I'm sorry—okay? I really am sorry, Mrs Mitchell.'

18

'So am I, Scott,' Madge said evenly, 'because I don't believe a word of it. I do not believe that *anyone* could be so naïve and insensitive.' She shrugged and assumed an attitude of grim determination. 'Well, I don't suppose it matters all that much in the long run. We Mitchells have been through rougher times than this, and no doubt we will survive your poison pen effort.'

Scott was stung by the barb. 'Oh, that's not fair . . .'

'Fair?' Madge studied him with open hostility. 'What would *you* know about fair? Just look at what your delinquent diary has done to Des and Daphne. Why don't you go over and talk to *them* about what's fair and what's not, and see how you get on?'

'Yeah, well, I only came over to say I'm sorry.' He decided it was time, if possible, to get off the subject. 'Is Charlene up?' he asked hopefully.

Madge stared at him. 'Scott,' she said crisply, 'I think that after what you have done, you had better forget about Charlene, don't you?'

'Come on.' Scott gestured helplessly. 'I just want to . . .'

'I mean it, Scott,' Madge broke in angrily. 'You are not to see her again.' With that, she closed the door firmly in his face.

If Madge Mitchell was hurt by the article, Charlene on the other hand was amused by it, as Scott learned later when he picked her up on her way home from her new job at the garage. 'Then you're not angry with me?' he asked in surprise.

'Of course not. I thought your story was a hoot.'

Scott was beginning to feel better. 'Well, what parts did you like best?'

She snuggled up against him. 'The bit about Charlotte, the beautiful daughter.'

'That was supposed to be about you,' Scott said shyly.

'Really?' She stared up at him with big, wondering eyes. 'Honestly? No kidding?' Scott could tell that she was teasing him. She became mock-serious. 'If it wasn't, I would have brained you.' She sighed wistfully. 'And I thought it

19

was really romantic, the way you described us as Romeo and Juliet. It made me feel special.'

That part had come easily to him; there had been no divergences from the truth when he had written about himself and Charlene. 'You *are* special,' he said in barely more than a whisper as he stopped the car at the end of Ramsay Street.

They kissed gently, sweetly. 'Mum has banned me from ever seeing you again,' Charlene said.

'Then you had better close your eyes.'

They kissed again, and again. 'I think she means it this time,' Charlene said with a sigh.

'I did try to apologise,' Scott said ruefully. 'But she wouldn't listen to me.'

'She'll get over it. Give her a bit of time.'

If Charlene was so sure that her mother would simmer down in time, that probability was far less certain with the formidable Mrs Mangel who at that moment, having barged into the Robinson house with a copy of the *Erinsborough News* clutched in her hand, was angrily denouncing Scott, whose *tawdry* piece of gutter journalism had cast aspersions on her good name throughout the length and breadth of Erinsborough, to his grandmother.

Mrs Mangel was devastated. The damage Scott's article would do to her good name in the community could well be irreparable, and she intended to take legal action. Why, the boy had virtually accused her of murdering her husband.

It was true that the article had highlighted the mysterious circumstances surrounding the sudden disappearance of Mrs Mangel's husband—and to a large extent it was Mrs Mangel's own fault that there had been so much speculation about it. She said nothing about it, and was evasive when questions were put to her about it; her behaviour had been decidedly strange—and when, fired by the spirit of investigation, Jane, Kelly and Charlene had unearthed his belongings which Mrs Mangel had buried in her back yard, it seemed only natural that speculation should have become rife. It was also natural that Scott should have drawn upon this when writing about Mrs Mangel, who was now claiming to the long-suffering Helen Daniels that it was all lies, lies, and it was really about time that she cleared up this matter of her disappearing husband once and for all.

Of course, she hadn't murdered him, she declared; the truth was much less dramatic than that; he had simply run away with some young Jezebel he had been carrying on with for many years before Mrs Mangel had found out and ordered him from the house. It had been a great shock to her; she hadn't acted in a rational way, and it had been under that strain, and not wishing to be reminded in any way of her errant spouse, she had buried his belongings in the back yard. Having delivered herself of this confession, still indignant and vowing vengeance against Scott for having committed the neighbourhood suspicions to print, she flounced out of the house.

'I didn't know,' Scott said weakly when Helen told him later of her encounter with the furious Mrs Mangel.

'No one of us did,' Helen said sharply. 'But would that have changed anything? Published and be damned—wasn't that your attitude?'

Scott looked at her helplessly; he wasn't sure any more what the answer was. All he did know was that he made one hell of a mess of things.

When Jim Robinson arrived home from work that evening, he found Scott slumped dejectedly on the living room sofa with his guitar across his knees. 'Ah, there you are,' he said. 'I expected to find you hard at work, slaving over the typewriter, churning out your next piece of character assassination.'

But Scott was feeling too miserable to rise to his father's sarcasm. 'Yeah . . . well . . . I decided to give it a break for a while,' he muttered.

'Good.' Jim nodded, then moved into the kitchen. Pushing himself up from the sofa, Scott followed him. 'Sandwich?' Jim asked.

Scott shook his head. 'Thanks, but it would stick in my throat right now.'

Jim turned from the refrigerator and regarded him quizzically. 'What's wrong?'

Scott felt the need to unburden himself. 'Dad, they were only meant to be entertaining stories,' he said unhappily. 'But everyone is taking them so personally.'

'Well, your grandmother and I *did* warn you,' Jim quietly reminded him.

'I know, I know. You were right.' Scott smiled bleakly. 'I guess I'm not the hot-shot author I thought I was,'

'Well, at least you've admitted you were wrong.' Jim seemed pleased by his son's change of attitude. 'Even if it is a little late. But as far as other people's opinions are concerned, I wouldn't worry too much. A few apologies, and a bit of time—the whole thing will blow over.'

Scott hoped he was right, but it wasn't the end of it—not just yet. 'Today was bad,' he said gloomily, 'but there's still one more story to come.'

'Oh?' Jim raised his eyebrows. 'Who's in the firing line this time?'

'We are. You, Paul, Gran, the works . . . but mainly Paul.' Jim's expression darkened; he made a gesture of exasperation. 'Dad, I didn't write it to upset anyone,' Scott said. 'But the way everyone has reacted to my other stories . . .' He shook his head helplessly. 'What am I going to do?'

'Speak to the editor,' Jim replied. 'Convince him not to print the story.'

That was more easily said than done. 'But I tried with those other stories . . .'

'Maybe he'll listen if both of us go down there,' Jim said.

Maybe . . . Scott though they would have a better chance; his father could be very persuasive when he set his mind to it. He suddenly realised how much he needed his father in a crisis, and that he had some way to go yet before he could properly shoulder the burden of responsibility.

'We'll have to give back the money you've been paid for the article,' Jim observed.

'Fair enough.'

'And when we get that article back, I don't want to read

it. I don't want anyone in this house to read it. You're the only who knows what it contains, and I think it's better if it stays that way.'

It was just as Scott wished it himself. There was something else on his mind. 'Dad?'

'Yes, son?'

'I've been thinking,' Scott said. 'Something I've been working up to. I've decided to go back to school.'

Jim beamed proudly and clasped his son's shoulder. 'Good on you, mate,' he said.

Two

Coming almost on top of Madge's divorce, here was Harold Bishop again. It was like an omen. Poor Harold.

'I must say, you've hardly changed in twenty years,' Harold said.

Madge wished she could say the same about him. He had been so handsome as a young man. Now, although he was still not bad looking, he had become rather . . . portly. 'More cake, Harold?'

'Thank you, but I shouldn't.'

'Coffee?'

'No, thank you.'

'There's some chicken casserole in the oven,' Madge offered. 'Perhaps you would like some of that.'

Harold shook his head. 'Well, actually, I don't eat meat.'

Madge looked at him in surprise. 'You're a vegetarian?'

'And much healthier for it. The cake was very nice.'

He had always been the perfect gentleman. He had been steady, reliable, with lovely manners and a bright future ahead of him. Madge's mum had thought he was the cat's whiskers. Then Fred Mitchell, who could charm the fillings out of one's teeth, had come along and Harold had suddenly seemed quite dull in comparison. But, as Madge was the first to acknowledge, common sense flies right out the window when one is young and in love. She had often wondered what life would have been like if she had married Harold Bishop instead of the charming and totally unreliable Fred Mitchell, who had finally made a goat of himself by running off with a woman young enough to be his daughter.

'Perhaps a glass of port then?'

'Oh no.' Harold's eyes widened behind his spectacles. 'I don't touch alcohol.'

Madge approved of that. 'How long are you staying in town?' she asked.

Harold was sitting rather primly on the edge of the arm-chair opposite her. From the time of his telephone call she had been quite chirpy at the prospect of seeing him again. She had baked a cake and taken a considerable amount of trouble over her appearance. She had even brought out her best china. 'Ah . . . yes . . . well now, that's in the lap of the gods,' Harold replied. 'Now that I've sold the stock and station agency, I'm looking for something different. That's why I came south. It's possible I may even stay here in Erinsborough.'

That sounded highly promising. 'That would be nice,' Madge remarked.

Harold glanced at his watch. 'I think I should be going. It has been a long and tiring day.'

'I'm sure,' Madge said sympathetically. 'All that travel-ling. Where are you staying?' she asked as Charlene came into the room.

'Lassiter's,' Harold told her. 'It's just a stroll down the road. Nice place, but a little on the pricey side.'

'That's Paul Robinson,' Charlene observed. 'He runs the place. But we can't complain though. Mum works there.'

Madge wished she hadn't said that; she was quite certain that Harold wouldn't approve if he was to learn that she worked there as a barmaid. 'Oh really?' Harold was looking at her with interest. 'What do you do there?'

'Ah . . . yes . . .' Madge thought quickly. 'I'm on the retail side of things.' She got off the subject of her involve-ment in the day-to-day running of the Lassiter Hotel com-plex. 'Yes, I suppose Paul does charge that little bit extra, but it serves to maintain the standard of the clientele.' She smiled warmly at the man opposite her. 'People like your-self, Harold.'

Harold smiled back at her. Charlene smiled at them both; she was taking a proprietary interest in this encounter after so many years between her mother and the guy who had brought her flowers and danced with her when she was a girl of about Charlene's own age. 'Oh, thank you, Madge,' Harold said, rising to his feet. 'I hope I'll be seeing more of you while I'm here.'

'Yes, of course.' Madge moved with him to the front door. 'Perhaps you would care to join us for lunch tomorrow,' she suggested. 'There's not a great deal to do in Erinsborough on a Sunday—apart from church, that is.'

'Oh?' Harold turned to her eagerly. 'May I join you?' Madge looked at him blankly, not sure what he was talking about. 'The church. You were planning to go, weren't you?'

Madge had been planning no such thing. 'Yes . . . yes, of course. That would be very nice. If you come here at, say, nine forty-five . . .'

'I'll be here,' Harold promised. He beamed at her. 'All right then, until tomorrow.'

'Yes, tomorrow.'

'And thank you for a delightful evening,' Harold said as he stepped out onto the porch.

'Goodnight, Harold,' Madge said, closing the door behind him.

'You weren't *really* planning on going to church tomorrow, were you, Mum?' Charlene asked her when she returned to the living room.

'Of course I was,' Madge replied firmly. 'It never does anyone harm to go to church occasionally.'

'You really like him, don't you? I mean, you brought out your best china.'

'If a person can't make a visitor feel welcome,' Madge said with feigned indifference, 'then there's not much charity left in the world.'

Harold called for her punctually in the morning. They sat beneath the stained glass windows of the church and listened to a sermon based on the injunction that a servant must be worthy of his hire, which Harold was later to praise as being perfectly relevant in this day and age. Oh yes, he declared, it was a perfectly inspiring declamation that had thundered down to them from the pulpit. They went back to Madge's place for lunch. Madge had thought of preparing a roast, but had remembered just in time that Harold was a vegetarian.

'I thought I would make a nice green salad, and pumpkin jardinière,' she said as they entered the house. 'It's a vegetarian dish.'

'Oh yes,' Harold said appreciatively. 'It's my favourite.'

'Good. Then you can tell me if I'm doing it right.'

When he discovered that they were not having their usual Sunday roast, Shane was rather put out. 'We're having something healthy instead,' Madge told her nephew. 'Baked pumpkin stuffed with cheese sauce and vegetables, and topped with toasted almonds. It's delicious.'

Harold nodded wisely. 'We Australians eat far too much red meat,' he pronounced.

Clad in a pair of old, oil-streaked overalls that were too large for her, Charlene came in from outside where she had been changing the oil in Scott Robinson's car. 'It's a healthy high-fibre diet,' Madge said to Shane. 'That's exactly what you need.'

'That's right, Shane,' Charlene remarked. 'Keep that in mind.'

Madge glared at her. 'And that's enough of *your* cleverness, young lady,' she said tartly. 'Now will you please go and change into something halfway decent.'

Charlene was regarding her mother's vegetable dish with some suspicion. 'What is it?'

'Good for you, Charlene,' Shane said with a smirk. 'Wholesome ingredients. Full of fibre.'

Charlene shook her head. 'None for me, thanks.'

Madge frowned at her. 'What?'

'Scott's taking me to the beach,' Charlene told her. 'We'll pick up something on the way.'

'But . . .'

'Not to worry,' Harold chimed in. 'We'll polish off her share. Won't we, Shane?'

'Yeah, sure,' Shane said doubtfully. 'No worries.'

After lunch, declared by Harold to be a huge success, which pleased Madge no end, they talked about the old days and the people they had known. Harold talked sadly of his wife who had died while their two children were still very young. 'It must have been terrible for you,' Madge said sympathetically.

'Oh, we managed,' Harold said with a dismissive wave of his hand. 'Fortunately, I had been careful with money, so I could afford the extra help.'

'All the same,' Madge said with a solemn shake of her head, 'it couldn't have been easy . . .'

'Nor is life in general *meant* to be easy.' Harold sighed, then changed the subject. 'I've been thinking, Madge,' he said. 'The hotel . . . well, hotels are a little impersonal, not to say expensive. So I thought it would be a better idea if I were to find a bedsitting room somewhere in the district . . . a boarding house . . . for the rest of my stay here.' He smiled a little tentatively at Madge who was sitting on the sofa beside him. 'You know, Madge, this place is becoming more attractive to me by the day.'

Madge knew from his tone, from his smile and the tenderness reflected in his eyes, that he could only be referring to her. She felt herself blushing a little. 'Oh dear,' she said in mild consternation. 'Perhaps you would like some herbal tea.'

Harold nervously cleared his throat. 'If you don't mind my saying, Madge . . . I think you have matured very gracefully. All the potential I saw in the young Madge Ramsay has been more than adequately realised. I think . . . I think you are a very beautiful person . . . in every way.'

Madge was embarrassed yet delighted at the same time; she didn't know where to look; her cheeks were positively burning now. 'Thank you, Harold,' she murmured. 'It has been a long time since anyone has said anything so . . . flattering to me.'

'Oh, it's not flattery,' Harold assured her. 'I hope you realise that.'

'Yes, of course.'

Harold cleared his throat again. 'I was wondering . . .'

'Yes, Harold?' she prompted when he hesitated.

'Wondering how you feel about me.'

Madge was startled by this question to which she had no ready answer. It was all too sudden; she had only just met him again after twenty years. 'Well . . .' She picked her words carefully; he was looking at her with so much hope in his eyes. 'You're a very charming man, Harold. Just as charming as you were all those years ago.'

'Yet you married Fred Mitchell.'

'And lived to regret it.'

There was a brief, thoughtful pause, then Harold said, 'I proposed to you once. Do you remember?'

'Of course I do.' Madge chuckled softly. 'No woman ever forgets a proposal.'

'I was very disappointed when you refused me.'

'I very nearly accepted.'

'Really?' Harold's eyes widened in surprise.

Madge laughed again. 'You had a very narrow escape, believe me.'

'But I didn't want to escape,' Harold said quietly. 'I still don't.'

'Oh, Harold.' Madge was flustered; she had no idea what was coming next. She rose abruptly to her feet. 'I'll bring you that tea.'

'Herbal teas.' If Harold was disappointed by Madge's reaction, he wasn't showing it. 'There's such a fascinating range of them. People just don't realise how many.'

'Oh yes?'

'There's camomile, rosehip . . .'

Madge hurried into the kitchen to put the water on.

Three

It was a ghastly predicament to be in; Helen Daniels was being torn apart by it. It was completely wrong, completely immoral. She was in love.

But it wasn't just the fact that she was in love, certainly no uncommon thing for a woman of her age, mother and grandmother of grown up children; the problem was that she was in love with the man her daughter intended to marry. And to make it worse, the man Rosemary intended to marry was in love with her. And Rosemary suspected nothing. It was an awful mess.

She had tried to resist it; she had distanced herself from it. But even after she had returned to Australia, Gerard had continued to bombard her with letters and long-distance telephone calls from America to declare his undying passion for her; he had been quite unnerving about it altogether. Now he was here, in Australia; Jim had just shown her the item in the newspaper about his one-man art exhibition which was opening in a few days, and noting her startled reaction, the sudden confusion which she had desperately tried to conceal, and being aware that she had become involved with a man while in America, had drawn his own conclusions.

As she explained it to Jim, she had met Gerard when she had gone to visit Rosemary in New York the previous year. Rosemary had been very busy at the time, which meant that Helen looked like being left to her own devices for the greater part of her stay. Then Gerard, who had just completed a painting commissioned by one of the major oil companies and so had plenty of time to spare, had taken her under his wing. As Rosemary's fiancé, he had considered it his duty—a most pleasurable one, he had assured her—to show her around the city. 'He took me to all the art galleries—the Metropolitan, the Guggenheim, the Frick, and . . . oh, dozens of small places in Greenwich Village and elsewhere.' He was older than Rosemary, and in each other's company they had discovered that they had a great deal in common. She went on quietly, her hands clasped together on her lap, a little more relaxed now that she had finally decided to confide in Jim who had pressed her into it really, knowing, as he put it, that she would feel much better once she had it all off her chest. 'Then, one afternoon we were to meet at the Whitney Museum in Madison Avenue. He was late. He was very late.' Helen recalled the anxiety she had felt during those forty minutes she had waited for him outside the museum, forcing herself to accept the possibility that he wouldn't come at all. She had felt so disappointed, so terribly let down. 'And then, suddenly, coming through the crowd, there he was. It was then that I knew. I was amazed—horrified even. But it didn't seem to matter. It was my secret, and something very private to me. Then . . .' she smiled wanly at the memory '. . . then a few days later, he was bringing me home in a taxi . . . and he took my hand, and we looked at each other . . . and I knew that he felt the same way. So I ran away. I packed my bags and came home without even consulting him. I thought that was going to be the end of it. But he keeps telephoning . . . and writing, and insisting that he loves me. And . . .' her eyes became misty; it was all very difficult '. . . I know it's true.'

'But the wedding,' Jim said softly. 'That's still going ahead by the sounds of it.'

The wedding . . . Rosemary and Gerard; Rosemary in white, and radiant, clutching a bouquet, hopelessly in love with the tall distinguished man beside her, just as her mother was hopelessly in love with him. Rosemary had already chosen the church in which they were to be married. 'Rosemary thinks it's going ahead,' Helen murmured. 'But

31

Gerard is as hurt as I am. He's been . . . well, I know he has been finding excuses . . .'

Jim had listened to her sympathetically; she was grateful to him for not taking a moral stance on the issue. 'Shouldn't you see him?' he suggested. 'Try to resolve this?'

'No.' Helen shook her head.

'Why not?'

Why not? The answer to that was simple. 'How can I choose between Gerard and my own daughter?'

'I see . . .'

It was inevitable that Gerard would try to see her while he was in the country. 'I suppose the simplest thing would be for me to go away for a few days,' Helen said thoughtfully. 'I've been promising myself a sketching trip to the mountains for some time now.'

Jim frowned at her. 'That's not the answer, Helen—and you know it. And anyway, you're probably worrying about nothing. If Rosemary is ready to set the wedding date, then Gerard has almost certainly made up his mind.'

'No, he hasn't.'

'Why not?'

'There are his letters . . .' She was becoming upset. 'I *know* he'll contact me.'

'Then I don't see you have any alternative,' Jim said.

There was another possibility. Helen looked hopefully up at her son-in-law who had begun to pace the living room floor. 'You could do it for me.' Jim stopped pacing and looked at her in surprise. 'You could explain,' she said. 'Tell him he should go ahead with the wedding.'

Jim shook his head doubtfully. 'Why should he take any notice of what *I* have to say?'

'If I won't see him,' Helen elaborated for him, 'he'll *have* to take notice of what you have to say. He has to be told it's over.' She regarded him intently. 'Jim, I'm the one who is coming between them. And if I'm determined not to see him, then that will prove it. Please, Jim . . .'

Jim was still clearly doubtful that it would work. 'I can't promise anything . . .'

'He'll listen to you,' Helen said urgently. 'I know he will. He *has* to listen to you.'

Jim thought about it. 'All right,' he said finally. 'I'll see him.'

Helen gave him a relieved smile. 'That's settled then. I'll try and find out where he's staying.'

It took quite a number of telephone calls, but she eventually did track down the hotel where Gerard was staying. She wrote the name of it on a sheet of paper which she handed to Jim at breakfast the following morning. Jim still didn't seem particularly happy about the project, but at Helen's insistence he renewed his promise to talk to Gerard some time during the day. At lunch time, Jim returned to the house to tell Helen that he had been out of luck. 'He was out,' he said. 'They had no idea where he was, or how long he would be. He could be out all day.'

He could even be on his way to see her. Helen was suddenly nervous. 'But if he comes here . . .'

'Helen,' Jim said reproachfully, 'this isn't like you at all.'

Helen couldn't help that; she was becoming quite agitated at the thought of Gerard possibly turning up on the doorstep any moment now. 'Jim, I love Rosemary, and I love Gerard. No matter what decision comes out of this, it means . . .' Her voice quavered a little; tears filled her eyes. '. . . it means heartbreak for me. I'm prepared for that. I'm . . . I'm the intruder.'

Jim patted her comfortingly on the shoulder. 'I do have an appointment this afternoon,' he said, 'but I could always cancel it.'

Helen knew she wasn't being fair to him. 'No, Jim. It was stupid of me. You were right. Just talking about it has helped.' She smiled a little shakily. 'No, you go ahead and keep your appointment. I'll be all right.'

'Are you sure?'

'Quite sure.'

'Well, the children will be here to keep you company.'

Helen gave a wry smile. They would hardly be any help to her. 'Go on,' she said. 'You'd better get moving if you want to keep that appointment.'

She was on her way back from the shops where she had picked up the ingredients for the casserole she was preparing for the family that evening, and had just turned into Ramsay Street when Scott came running towards her. 'Gran, you've got a visitor,' he called.

Helen stood motionless on the footpath with her shopping bag in her hand. 'What?'

'Gerard Singer,' Scott explained, pulling up in front of her. 'Rosemary's fiancé. I told him you wouldn't be long, that you'd only gone down to the shops.' Helen still didn't move. Suddenly feeling very weak and frightened, she stared at her grandson without really seeing him. All she could see were problems, difficulties, a great deal of unpleasantness. 'Come on, Gran,' Scott urged her. 'Gerard's waiting. He's probably getting a real earbashing right now from Lucy.'

Helen found her voice at last. 'Oh yes. I'd better go and see him.'

Scott was looking at her with concern. 'Is there anything wrong, Gran?'

'No, it's all right, Scott. There's nothing wrong.'

There was everything wrong. She had to face Gerard now. The moment she had been dreading had come. The man she loved, the man who loved her . . . She had to tell him now that her mind was made up, that there was to be no more deception . . .

As she entered the house, she could hear Gerard talking to Lucy in the living room. Apparently Lucy was showing him some of her grandmother's paintings for she heard him say in that softly modulated American voice of his, 'But if you do decide to take up painting and take after your grandmother . . . well, if you can produce anything like this, you'll hardly need any help from me.'

At the sound of his voice, so warm and vibrant, always reassuring, Helen began to tremble. She almost turned away, but then, taking a deep breath, forcing herself with an effort to some semblance of calm, she walked into the room just as Lucy was asking Gerard if he would like to see some of her own paintings.

34

'Ah . . . later, Lucy,' Gerard said, then seeing Helen in the doorway, rose to his feet. 'Oh, Helen, there you are.'

He was smiling at her—and how handsome he looked, how bronzed and distinguished. 'Hello, Gerard,' she greeted him as she advanced into the room with her hand outstretched. 'It's nice to see you again.'

He took her hand and pressed it gently. 'Guess what, Gran,' Lucy said, looking up at her with wide, expectant eyes. 'Mister Singer said he would help me with my painting.'

Gerard picked up one of her paintings from a stack against the wall. It was one of the seascapes. 'I was just saying she'll do very well, if she develops your style.'

Helen was annoyed with Lucy; she felt some vague sense of betrayal. 'Lucy,' she snapped, 'how many times have I told you not to touch my paintings?'

Gerard gestured apologetically. 'It was probably my fault . . .'

Helen ignored him; she was under a tremendous strain. 'Now you put them back in the bedroom where you found them,' she commanded Lucy in a brittle voice.

With a pout and a shrug of her shoulders, Lucy picked up the paintings and carried them out of the room. 'A nice kid,' Gerard observed after she had gone. 'She's very proud of you.'

Helen was determined to keep the conversation civil and on an even keel. 'How are the preparations for the exhibition coming along?' she asked.

'Very well, I think.' He studied her earnestly for a long moment. Helen was aware of the rapid beating of her heart, the warmth in her cheeks. 'I had to see you, Helen.'

'Please, Gerard.' Helen turned away from those compelling eyes of his. 'Not now.'

'I knew if I called you, you would find some way of stalling.'

'Gerry, you had no right to come here,' Helen said miserably.

'You wouldn't have seen me if I had left it up to you.'

35

That was perfectly true. 'There's no reason why I should.'

'Of course there is, Helen,' Gerard said intently. 'I needed to see you. And you know why.'

Helen sighed; she knew only too well. 'I have said all I wanted to say.'

They were keeping their voices low so that Lucy wouldn't hear them. 'You did, maybe,' Gerard said. 'But not me. That's why I kept calling you, and writing. And the last time we saw each other . . . well, there wasn't so much time to talk.'

'But what's to discuss?' Helen couldn't keep the bitterness out of her voice. 'You're engaged to my daughter.'

Gerard moved across the room to her. 'Are you going to deny how we feel about each other?' he demanded. 'I can't.'

Crossing to the sideboard, Helen picked up a photograph Rosemary had sent from America. It was a picture of a church built of grey stone and surrounded by well kept lawns and flowerbeds. She handed it to Gerard, who studied it with a puzzled frown. 'What's this?'

'It's the church in which Rosemary has decided to get married. On the back is a list of possible dates.'

'Yes . . .' Looking troubled, Gerard handed the photograph back to her. 'We did discuss wedding plans, but I had no idea she had taken it this far.'

'Well, she has,' Helen said. 'I think it's perfectly reasonable that a bride-to-be would want to know when . . .' there was a catch in her voice . . . 'when her family can get to the wedding.'

Gerard was staring into her eyes again; Helen could feel herself trembling again. 'I can't marry Rosemary,' he said with vibrant intensity. 'I love you, Helen—and I know you love me.'

Helen felt confused and weak; she tried desperately to find something to say, but no words would come. Nor could she find it within herself to resist him when he gently took her in his arms and kissed her. But then, as she could feel herself succumbing to the embrace, returning the kiss, almost melting in his arms, she did manage to summon the strength to break away from him. 'Please, Gerard,' she said a little breathlessly. 'Don't. Please go.'

She could see the hurt in his eyes. 'When Rosemary told me you had gone back to Australia,' he said unhappily, 'my first impulse was to come straight after you. Then I got to thinking that maybe you left because you didn't love me. And then I thought that perhaps my feelings for you might change.' With a grim little smile, he shook his head. 'But they didn't. That's why I'm here now.'

'I wish to goodness you weren't.' Helen blurted it out without really thinking.

'Is that the truth? Please, Helen, look at me.'

Reluctantly, Helen forced herself to look at him. 'All right. I *do* love you,' she conceded in a small, unhappy voice. 'But I don't matter. It's Rosemary who counts.'

'But why can't we just accept the way we feel?' Gerard queried with a plaintive edge to his voice. 'And do something about it?'

'What are you suggesting?' Helen's own voice became sharper. 'That I confess to my daughter that I'm in love with the man she's about to marry?'

'She'll find out sooner or later.'

'No, Gerry,' Helen said firmly. 'Because whatever I started with you, however unintentionally, I'm finishing it right now.'

'Then you're letting Rosemary's happiness get in the way of your own,' Gerard pointed out to her. 'You should be thinking of yourself for once.'

He was trying to make it easier for her, but it wouldn't work. 'If I choose you,' she said simply, 'I lose my daughter.'

Gerard frowned. 'Yes, I understand that, Helen,' he said slowly. 'But I'm not going to give you up so easily. Even if you don't change your mind, I can't marry Rosemary now.'

The tears welled up in Helen's eyes. 'I wish I had never met you,' she moaned.

'But I'll always be glad I met you.'

He was moving towards her to comfort her when she

suddenly became aware that Jim was standing in the doorway, watching them. She hadn't heard him come in. Then Gerard realised they were not alone; he stepped back. Helen quickly tried to compose herself. 'Oh Jim,' she said with a relieved smile. 'You're back early.'

'The meeting didn't take long.' Jim was looking curiously at Gerard. 'You must be Gerard,' he said, extending his hand. 'I'm Jim Robinson.'

'Hi there.' Gerard looked a little uncomfortable as he shook Jim's hand.

'Yes, I tried to reach you at your hotel this morning,' Jim told him.

'Really?' Gerard glanced apprehensively at Helen. 'Why was that?'

'I wanted to meet you,' Jim replied, 'and ask you to keep away from Helen.'

'What?' Gerard looked at Helen for an explanation.

'Jim knows,' she said. 'I told him.'

'I see.' Gerard turned back to Jim. 'I take it you don't approve.'

'I'm not taking sides,' Jim said evenly. 'I just know how Helen feels about it, that's all. And I think you need time to consider your position very carefully.'

Gerard shook his head. 'Helen doesn't need to consider at all,' he stated emphatically.

'I think maybe you should respect her wishes,' Jim suggested.

Helen was only just managing to hold back her tears. 'Gerry, I think you should go,' she said.

Gerard looked at her for a few moments, then gave a resigned shrug. 'Well, I know *I'm* not about to change my mind,' he said, moving to the door. 'You know where I am if you need me.' He nodded curtly to Jim. 'I'll see you around.'

'Goodbye,' Jim said as Helen finally yielded in the struggle to contain her tears.

When Rosemary telephoned that evening from New York, bubbling with excitement and full of plans, Helen found it almost impossible to keep up the charade, so emotionally drained was she after the encounter with Gerard. But she managed to come through, to sound cheerful enough. She told her daughter that Gerard had visited her that afternoon.

'Oh great,' Rosemary laughed. 'Did he say he missed me?'

'Yes, of course.' It was painful for Helen to have to lie like this. 'He misses you very much.'

Despite the great distance between them, Helen could hear the happiness in her daughter's voice, and once again found herself fighting back the tears. 'What with his work and mine,' Rosemary was saying, 'we hardly see each other. Still, all that will change once we're married.' Helen shook her head woefully as she blinked back the tears; it was more than she could bear. 'The next time you see him, Mum, would you tell him I love and miss him terribly?'

'Yes . . . I'll do that.'

'I'm very happy, Mum.'

'Yes, dear, I know . . .'

The following morning, Gerard turned up at the house again and insisted that Helen have lunch with him. His exhibition was opening that night, and he was a little nervous. 'I was hoping you might take pity on me,' he said. 'Otherwise I will be going crazy, sitting in that hotel room and praying I won't be a complete flop.'

Helen demurred; she looked for excuses. 'I don't think I can . . .'

'Please, Helen.' He took her hand and stared imploringly into her eyes. She could already feel herself weakening. 'Just this once. Besides, there's something I want to show you.'

In the end, unable to resist him, she agreed, but she wasn't happy about it; she just wished he wouldn't do this to her. It wasn't at all fair; it wasn't making matters any easier.

In the coffee shop, she sat uncomfortably opposite him. She wasn't hungry; she had just ordered coffee. Saying he wasn't very hungry either, Gerard had also ordered coffee. 'I'm sorry about turning up like that,' he said. 'But I just

39

had to see you.' He put down his cup after taking a sip of coffee. 'I've been doing a lot of thinking, Helen,' he continued earnestly, 'and I have decided there's only one way out of this mess.' He leaned forward across the table, and Helen dreaded what was coming next. 'I love you, Helen,' he said softly but intensely, 'and I'm going to tell Rosemary that.'

Helen was horrified at the thought. Her hand jerked and almost knocked over her coffee cup. 'No, Gerry, you mustn't do that. Not now. You must give yourself more time. I'm sure that once you get back to America . . .'

'I'll feel exactly as I do now,' he broke in. 'Look . . .' He reached into his jacket pocket and produced an envelope. 'I'd like you to read this.' He held the envelope out to her. After a moment's hesitation, Helen took it from him. 'I've tried to be as kind as I know how,' Gerard said.

Almost fearfully, Helen took the letter from the envelope and began to read it. He was right; he had been kind, but devastating nevertheless. In his firm handwriting, he had written about love and honesty—and then Helen found the words blurring in front of her eyes. 'But you can't break off your engagement like this,' she said weakly. 'You haven't been . . . totally honest about your reasons for not wanting to marry her.'

'I didn't think I had the right,' he said. 'Rosemary is your daughter. I thought you would want to tell her yourself . . . in your own way.'

Helen handed the letter back to him. 'I don't want to tell her at all.'

Gerard gestured awkwardly. 'Perhaps I could have phrased that better,' he murmured as he replaced the letter in his pocket, then leaned forward again. 'Look, Helen . . . none of us wanted this to happen, but it has. I love you, and I know you love me—and if I marry Rosemary, the three of us will be unhappy. Can't you see that?'

But all Helen could see was that as matters now stood she was desperately unhappy, anyway, and that whichever way it went she would still be desperately unhappy. 'Yes,

I can,' she whispered in anguish. 'But it doesn't make things any easier.'

Gerard nodded solemnly. 'I'll still be breaking it off with Rosemary, whatever happens between us two.'

'Yes . . . if you must.' Helen sighed. He had made up his mind; it was his own decision. 'But don't send her that letter. It's too cruel.'

'Yes, perhaps that would be taking the easy way out,' he acknowledged. He smiled grimly. 'All right then. I'll do it your way. I'll tell her the next time I see her.'

Helen stared worriedly down at her coffee which was getting cold. Her world was slowly falling apart. She still sensed disaster.

It seemed that matters were going to come to a head much sooner than she had anticipated, as she discovered that afternoon when Paul informed her that Rosemary had just telephoned from the States to say that she was on her way to the airport and would be arriving in the country the following morning. 'Tomorrow?' Helen was quick to hide the shock the news had given her. 'Oh, that's wonderful,' she said, with as much enthusiasm she could muster under the circumstances.

Partly, Rosemary's visit was prompted by the affairs of her international corporation, the Australian end of which, centred around the Lassiter Hotel complex, was handled by her nephew and Helen's grandson, Paul Robinson. But more than that, she explained to Helen in delight after they had picked her up at the airport, she had really been missing Gerard too much to be away from him a moment longer.

Gerard had come with them to the airport. 'Didn't you think Rosemary would expect me to meet her?' he asked when Helen had shown surprise at his insistence in joining them.

'Yes, of course.' Helen had laughed a little bitterly. 'The loving fiancé.'

'Don't be like that, Helen, please.'

Seeing the pain in his eyes, Helen had relented and apologised. 'When are you going to tell her?' she had asked after a brief pause.

'Well, I did say the sooner the better,' Gerard had murmured uncomfortably. 'But I can't exactly break it to her as she steps off the plane.'

'It's a pity you have to break it at all,' Helen had remarked a little severely.

And now, here she was, hugging them all, deliriously happy to be back again, to be with the most wonderful man in the world, she declared, taking Gerard's arm and looking up at him with eyes that were slightly misty. And the best mother in the world, she added with a fond smile at Helen who at that moment was filled with self-disgust.

'You've no idea how good it is to be back,' Rosemary said after she had taken her bags into the room that had been set aside for her and returned to the living room where Helen and Gerard were waiting for her with increasing apprehension. 'Oh, and I've got a million and one things to do before the wedding.'

'There's plenty of time,' Helen said with a quick worried glance at Gerard. 'You've just got off the plane. Why don't you wait a while, until you're settled in a little more?'

'Oh Mum.' Rosemary laughed. Even after the long plane journey, she still looked cool and unruffled; she looked extremely buoyant and happy. 'This is *me* you're talking to. When I'm happy, I'm busy. When I'm busy . . .' she smiled broadly at Gerard who shifted a little on the sofa . . . 'I'm happy.'

'That's true,' Helen said as she stood up. 'I'll leave you two alone. You must have things to talk about.' She looked meaningfully at Gerard.

'No,' Gerard said quickly. 'Don't go just yet.'

'No, not yet, Mum.' Rosemary took her mother's arm. 'There's something very important I have to ask you.' She turned to Gerard who wasn't looking happy at all. 'And this involves you, too, darling.'

Helen laughed somewhat nervously. 'Well? What is it?'

'It's something I've been thinking about for weeks, Mum.' Rosemary suddenly seemed a little flustered. 'I'd like you . . . well, would you be my matron-of-honour?'

On top of everything else . . . Helen was dismayed by

the request; it was something she hadn't anticipated. She tried to think of an excuse to get out of it. 'Well . . . it would be different, I suppose,' she murmured. 'But there are our clothes . . . How could we possibly co-ordinate?'

That was no problem for Rosemary. 'I've brought cuttings of the material with me,' she announced chirpily. 'I have been dying to show you. You'll love them.' She gave her fiancé another happy smile. 'Darling, make her say yes while I'm getting them.' She ran excitedly out of the room.

'I'll tell her now,' Gerard muttered determinedly to Helen after she had gone.

Helen looked at him in some surprise; she had half-expected him to find another excuse to put it off. 'Are you sure?'

'I've never been so sure of anything in my life,' Gerard said with an anguished sigh. 'I want to talk to her alone, Helen.'

'Yes, perhaps that would be better.'

She couldn't stay in the house; she needed to be alone. Quietly letting herself out by the front door, she began to walk. She walked as far as the park where she sat on a bench beside the lake. Her thoughts were racing, in a turmoil, as she tried to imagine the scene that was taking place back at the house. Gerard would try to be calm and cool about it, of course, as he appealed to Rosemary to see his decision in a reasonable light. But Helen couldn't see her doing that; she would be understandably angry, bitter and humiliated. Helen could only feel so terribly unhappy for her.

By the time she returned to the house about an hour later, Gerard had gone. The house was silent. Helen moved warily into the living room. 'Rosemary?' she called. 'Rosemary, where are you?'

Then Rosemary appeared in the kitchen doorway. Helen could tell that she had been crying. 'Where did you go?' Rosemary asked in a listless voice.

'Gerard said he wanted to talk with you,' Helen replied. 'It sounded important. I thought it would be easier if I made myself scarce.'

'Talk with me?' Rosemary's laugh was hard and bitter. 'Oh yes, he wanted to talk with me all right.' Her face began to crumple; her eyes filled with tears. 'Oh, Mum . . . What am I going to do? He said he loves someone else. He has called off the engagement.'

'Oh darling, I'm sorry.' Moving across the room to her daughter, Helen took her in her arms and held her tightly. 'So *very* sorry,' she whispered in total anguish as Rosemary began to weep convulsively in her arms.

After she had quietened down, and Helen had made some coffee, Rosemary began to pace the living room floor while Helen sat quietly, watching her and feeling too guilty to offer her more than the occasional word of comfort. 'Do you know what the worst thing is?' Rosemary exclaimed. 'It's that I feel so stupid. Gerard has been conning me all this time. I mean, this affair of his must have been going on for ages.' Helen said nothing; Rosemary took another turn around the room and continued. 'Oh, I know we didn't have the most passionate relationship in the world. But was that my fault? He was away with his exhibitions and his teaching assignments just as much . . . no, more than I was occupied with the business. But even so, I thought we had something really special. I thought this one was for keeps.' She laughed harshly and shook her head in disbelief. 'Oh boy, how stupid can you get?'

'Please, darling,' Helen murmured, 'try and calm down . . .'

'No, I'm good at what I do,' Rosemary said, forcefully overriding her. 'People respect me. They say I have a nose for a good deal. then along comes Gerard Singer and knocks me for six.' She turned to look squarely at her mother. 'But why did he wait to come to Australia before telling me?' Helen had no answer to that. 'Yes . . . yes,' Rosemary went on with an unpleasant smile. 'She's bound to be one of his arty set. A trendy little redhead who can spout off on cue about the philosophy of art . . .'

'Darling, why don't you lie down for a while?' Helen suggested. 'You'll feel better.'

'Mum,' Rosemary said with quiet bitterness. '*Nothing*

can make you feel better when you know someone has made a fool of you.'

'But you need your rest,' Helen insisted. 'You've had a long journey. Perhaps . . . after you've had a rest . . . we can talk about Gerard then.'

Rosemary was now looking very tired. 'All right,' she sighed. 'I suppose you're right.' She headed for the door, then stopped and turned back to Helen. 'Mum?'

'Yes, dear?'

'Thanks,' Rosemary smiled tightly. 'I don't think I could see this through without you.'

Oh God . . . Helen forced herself to smile back at her daughter who had just been so deeply hurt because of her. 'You go and have your rest now,' she urged.

Helen had said goodbye to Gerard. They had had lunch then parked beside the lake. It had been a meeting fraught with emotion; Helen was still feeling quite drained by it. Gerard had told her, as they sat in the car and stared out over the water, that he couldn't go back to Rosemary because he would be living a lie if he did. 'And if I can't have you . . .'

'Please, Gerry, you promised . . .'

'Yes, I did. I'm sorry. Are you going to tell her about us?'

'I don't know. I can't see that it would help.'

'Perhaps not,' Gerard had said wistfully. 'Perhaps honesty is not always the best policy after all.'

And then they had parted, and Helen had been unable to hold back her tears. They had kissed, and Gerard had told her that he would always love her, which had made the parting even more unbearable. Then he had gone, and Helen had been left alone.

That was how it might have remained if Rosemary hadn't been so determined to discover the identity of the woman who had replaced her. 'I must know,' she insisted. 'Don't you see? That's the worst thing about it—not knowing who she is. I mean, what does she have that I don't have? Is she younger, older, prettier, smarter? I wish I knew.'

'Would it really help?' Helen asked nervously.

'Yes, it would,' Rosemary replied. 'Definitely it would. Because I can't hate Gerard, no matter what. And I want to hate *her*, because she is the one who is responsible for all this. But I can't despise a woman I can't picture.'

Through all this, a violent struggle was going on inside Helen. She didn't know what to do—whether to come out with it now and tell her everything, throw herself on her daughter's mercy, or . . . 'Perhaps it's better not to know,' she said quietly.

For the next few days, Rosemary involved herself wholeheartedly in the affairs of her company, which was something of a relief for Helen as it seemed to be taking her mind off Gerard, although she was more snappy than usual and was inclined to take things out on Paul much more than necessary. Gerard had returned to America, and Rosemary herself would be going in a few days. Then, one morning at breakfast, when Lucy asked Rosemary if she would send her stamps from New York, Helen received a fright.

'Of course, dear,' Rosemary promised her small niece. 'There are some very fine stamps in America.'

'Oh yes, I know,' Lucy said. 'I've seen them on the letters Gran has been getting from America.'

Helen tensed and exchanged a worried glance with Jim. Rosemary looked interested. 'Oh? I didn't know you had friends in America, Mum.' She laughed at Helen's obvious discomfort. 'Who is it? A secret admirer?'

'No, no,' Helen said quickly. 'Just a friend I met while I was over there.'

That day, Rosemary had promised to take Lucy to the dentist while Helen caught up with some outstanding work at the office. When Jim telephoned her and asked her to come home immediately, Helen's first thought was that there had been some complication with regard to Lucy's dental treatment. When she asked if this was so, Jim shocked her by telling her that it was nothing like that, it was Rosemary. 'She has found out about you and Gerard,' he said. 'She's getting ready to leave.'

'My God!' Helen exclaimed in horror. 'But how . . . ?'

'Lucy showed her some stamps when they came home from the dentist's,' Jim, told her. 'Look, Helen, just get home. I'll explain later.'

'All right.' Helen was battling hard to keep control. 'Tell her to wait for me.'

'She won't. She's extremely upset. Your only hope is to catch her before she goes.'

'I'm coming now.' Helen hurriedly replaced the receiver.

But by the time she reached the house, Rosemary had gone. She was moving into Lassiter's Hotel, Jim explained, until it was time to catch her flight. 'Does she hate me very much?' Helen asked miserably, then answered her own question when Jim didn't reply. 'Of course she does. Why wouldn't she?'

'She's angry,' Jim said awkwardly. 'She's confused. Give her some breathing space. She'll come round in time.'

'Perhaps I should go to Lassiter's and see her,' Helen said. 'She might be willing to talk to me by now.'

Jim shook his head. 'I'd leave it for a while if I were you. You're emotionally wrung out, and my guess is that Rosemary is as well. So have some rest,' he suggested. 'You'll be able to cope better then.'

In a strange and awful way, Helen was relieved that the decision had been taken out of her hands at least. She supposed it was inevitable that Rosemary would have discovered the truth sooner or later. If—as she was to learn from Jim—Lucy hadn't shown Rosemary the American stamps on the envelopes of the letters Helen had received from Gerard; if she hadn't recognised the handwriting, then, her curiosity ignited, read the letters declaring his love for her mother, she would have found out in some other way. Or so Helen reasoned after Jim had explained to her how Rosemary had come to discover the bitter truth. She hadn't given the letters, which she kept in the drawer of her bureau, another thought, not even when Lucy had mentioned the American stamps at breakfast that morning, which should have alerted her to do something about them.

'Yes, things may be a little less black for both of us if we let ourselves calm down a bit,' she said. 'You know, half of me wants to put it off as long as possible, while the other half . . .' she sighed . . . 'oh, I just want to get it over and done with.' She looked bleakly at her son-in-law. 'What am I supposed to say when I *do* see her? That I'm terribly sorry? That I didn't mean to come between her and Gerard?'

'Come on.' Jim tried to be reassuring. 'It's not a crime to fall in love.'

'Oh . . .' Helen smiled sorrowfully . . . 'I was carried away, like a silly schoolgirl. I let this thing with Gerry get completely out of hand.'

Jim still tried to make her see that it wasn't nearly as foolish as she was making out. 'Just because you're older than Rosemary that doesn't mean you're incapable of falling in love.'

'No. But not with my daughter's fiancé.' Jim said nothing. Helen went on. 'You know, for a fleeting moment in New York, I was deliriously happy. I was a fool. I should have got out while the going was good.'

'Rosemary will understand. She's an intelligent woman.'

In time; the wounds would probably heal in time, but there would still be scars. 'Oh, *damn* Gerry!' Helen exclaimed bitterly. 'I just wish to goodness that I had never laid eyes on him.'

Four

Henry was coming out of gaol tomorrow, and he needed help. He needed money. 'Oh, I might have expected that,' Madge said without enthusiasm when Charlene broke the news to her. 'All right, how much?'

Charlene had just returned from visiting her brother in prison. 'It's to pay off some gambling debts.'

'I might have known,' Madge said with a weary sigh. 'How much does he want? Fifty dollars? A hundred?'

Charlene steeled herself for the blast she knew was to come. 'A thousand.'

'A thous . . .'

'He has to have it by tomorrow morning,' Charlene went on quickly. 'Otherwise he will never get out of prison alive.'

Madge was staring at her in disbelief. 'A thousand dollars?' she whispered. 'What on earth does he think he's doing?'

Charlene shrugged. 'It's one way of passing the time when you're in gaol,' she observed.

'He could have read books. Or studied. Or something.'

'You know what Henry's like.'

'Oh yes, I know what Henry's like.' Madge shook her head emphatically. 'I'm sorry, Charlene, but the answer is no.'

'But, Mum . . .' Charlene was shocked by Madge's blunt refusal to help her only son in a time of crisis. 'I wasn't kidding. They'll take him apart.'

'Don't be silly, Charlene.' Madge was resolutely standing her ground.

'He wouldn't *lie* about it, Mum.' There was an edge of desperation in Charlene's voice.

'He's done nothing but lie since the day he could talk,' Madge said angrily. 'He just wouldn't *know* what the truth was.' She shook her head again. 'No, this is just another scheme to get my money from me—and it's not going to work. And in any case, I've got news for the pair of you— I just don't have any money.'

'Oh, yes you do,' Charlene was quick to remind her. 'There's that five thousand dollars in your investment account.'

'You're not getting your hands on that,' Madge snapped. 'I've put that money away for my old age—and if you think I'm giving that to Henry, then you've got another think coming.'

Charlene was bitterly disappointed by her mother's attitude. 'I might have known you wouldn't help him,' she cried. 'You never have.'

'That's not true, Charlene. I've done everything I can to help him.'

The back door opened. 'What's going on?' Shane asked, glancing curiously from one tense face to the other as he came into the kitchen.

'Henry has been gambling,' Madge told him grimly. 'He owes some people a lot of money.'

'How much?'

'A thousand dollars.'

Shane whistled softly. Certain that her cousin would support her, Charlene made another appeal to Madge. 'He's really scared, Mum. They'll kill him if he doesn't pay.'

'Yeah?' Shane was obviously dubious. 'I bet he's scared— too scared to come home and face the music.'

This wasn't the reaction Charlene had expected from him. 'Shane, it's not a joke,' she reproached him. 'I thought you would understand.'

'I do, I do,' Shane returned quickly. 'But he's a big boy now—and it's not as if Aunty Madge hasn't bailed him out a hundred times already. He has to stand on his own two

50

feet.' He looked across at his aunt. 'You're not going to give him that money, are you?'

'Of course not.'

Charlene was furious. She had never heard anything so callous, so criminally cold-hearted. Fighting to keep a check on her temper, she swung on her heel and stomped out into the hall towards the front door. 'Where are you going?' Madge called after her.

'If *you* won't give him the money,' Charlene shouted back at her, 'then I will have to figure out a way to get it myself.' She slammed the front door behind her.

She needed to talk to someone. She found Daphne Clarke at work in the coffee shop. 'Look,' she said, after having explained the situation to her, 'I know Henry has given Mum heaps, he has always been a bit of a problem—but you'd think she would help him out just this once.'

'Just this once?' Daphne looked at her doubtfully.

'All right.' Charlene gestured impatiently. 'Maybe it's not the first time he has asked her for a loan. But he's desperate, Daphne.'

'That's probably what he said the last time.'

Charlene glared at her accusingly. 'Whose side are you on?' she demanded.

'I'm not taking sides.'

'Look . . .' Charlene was beginning to think she had made a mistake if she had expected at least a sympathetic hearing from Daphne. Henry's only got me and Mum to turn to when he needs us.'

'Madge loves both of you, Charlene,' Daphne said quietly.

'Then she's got a funny way of showing it.'

'And Henry's not doing such a good job of showing it, either, is he?' Daphne countered. 'If he cared about your mother,' she went on evenly, 'I mean, if he *really* cared, he wouldn't have done this in the first place.'

It had been a mistake. Even Daphne was against Henry. Bitter tears pricked Charlene's eyes. 'I bet *you* wouldn't turn your back on your son—if you had one—if you knew he was in trouble.'

'I hope I never find myself in that position,' Daphne said calmly. 'Charlene, your mother is doing her best—she knows how—and if she thinks it's better that Henry takes responsibility for his gambling debts, then you have to respect her decision. She knows her own mind—you have to give her credit for that.'

But Charlene wasn't seeing it that way. 'It's not as if she doesn't have the money. And Henry would pay her back—I know he would.'

'How many times has he told her that before?'

Charlene was forced to acknowledge the fact that it had been more than once. 'Yeah, well . . .'

'Maybe Madge is right this time,' Daphne said. 'He can't go on relying on her forever, now can he?'

The fact that Charlene had to admit that Daphne was right only made it worse for her. She didn't know what to do; she was absolutely desperate. She returned home to find Shane with tears in his eyes as he chopped up an onion in preparation for dinner. 'How come Aunty Madge doesn't cry when she chops up onions?' he asked as she came in through the back door.

'She puts them under water.' She looked around for her mother. 'Where is she, by the way?'

'She went to see Henry.'

'What did she do that for?' Charlene was put out by the news. 'The last thing he needs is another lecture.'

Shane threw down the knife with which he had been chopping up the onion and the other vegetables that were piled up on the board beside him. 'Now you just listen to me for a minute . . .'

Charlene didn't want to listen to him. She turned away from him. 'Why should I? You're always taking her side.'

'I'm tired of the way you treat her,' Shane said in annoyance. 'The way you expect her to come running every time you and Henry whistle. She's got a life of her own to lead, you know.'

Swinging back to face him, Charlene tried another tack. 'If Danny got himself into trouble, you'd help him out, wouldn't you?'

'Danny wouldn't be dumb enough to end up in gaol for pinching things,' Shane replied, 'and then turn round and expect me to pay his gambling debts. I wouldn't do it, anyway.'

'Some brother you are,' Charlene muttered in disgust as the front door closed and footsteps were heard in the hall.

Madge looked quite pale and shaken as she came slowly into the room. Shane moved across to her. 'Aunty Madge, are you okay?'

'Yes, I'm all right.' Madge put her bag down on the kitchen table. She seemed very far away.

'I hope Henry is, too,' Charlene remarked drily, 'after copping a mouthful from you.'

'You'll cop a fistful from me if you don't shut up, Charlene,' Shane growled, then turned back to Madge who had slumped heavily onto a chair. 'What did Henry have to say for himself?' he asked her.

Madge sighed. 'He was telling the truth,' she said distantly. 'He has already had a beating.'

Her fears having been vindicated, Charlene looked from her mother to Shane. 'Now do you both believe me?' she demanded urgently.

Shane still didn't seem to be sure. 'That's what he told you, is it?' he asked Madge.

'Bruised ribs,' Madge said with an unhappy nod. 'He showed me. And he'll get worse tomorrow if he doesn't come up with the money.' There were tears in her eyes as she regarded them bleakly. 'What am I going to do?'

'You can get the money out of your account,' Charlene told her. 'Can't you?'

'I don't know whether I can, Charlene,' Madge said after considering this for a moment. 'It's an investment account. The money is supposed to be in there for three years.'

'Then it looks as if Henry is out of luck, doesn't it?' Shane said with a shrug.

Charlene was close to panic. 'But we can't just sit here and let him be beaten up again,' she cried desperately.

'It might be the only way he'll learn anything,' Shane

observed with brutal frankness. 'Talking to him hasn't been too effective, has it?'

'Mum, don't listen to him,' Charlene cried in agitation. At that moment she could quite easily have beaten Shane to a pulp for his unfeeling attitude—or made the attempt in any event. 'Henry could be *killed* if you don't do something.'

Madge had gone next door to discuss the problem with Des Clarke when Harold Bishop called at the house to see her. Sensing a potential ally, Charlene began to fuss over her mother's old flame who had recently moved into the district. She asked him if he would like to stay for dinner; they were having chops, but Shane had prepared enough vegetables to satisfy his vegetarian tastes. When Harold said that would be lovely, Charlene smiled sweetly at Shane who was watching her with the utmost suspicion and asked him to set another place at the table.

She had made Harold comfortable in the living room. 'Have you heard from your children lately?' she asked after Shane returned to the kitchen.

'Well . . .' Harold smiled at her placidly. 'David is still working very hard,' he said. 'Oh, and yes, I finally received a postcard from Kerry. She's having a wonderful time in Europe.'

Charlene was showing great interest. 'You must worry about her being so far away'

'Oh yes, of course. There are so many pitfalls, dangers . . . terrorist attacks. It's very worrying.'

'But if anything did happen to her,' Charlene persisted, 'you would do anything to help, wouldn't you?'

'Yes, of course.'

'And Kerry would know that.'

'Certainly.'

'Charlene,' Shane called from the kitchen. 'Could you come here for a moment please.'

Excusing herself to Harold, Charlene moved into the kitchen where Shane was looking very stern. 'What's wrong?' she asked innocently.

'Just cut it out, will you.'

'What am I doing?'

'You know what you're doing. You're getting Harold all sympathetic so that both of you can gang up on your Mum.'

Charlene was just about to protest at this when the back door opened and Madge entered with a deeply preoccupied expression. 'How did you go, Mum?' Charlene asked her hopefully.

'I have to give a month's notice to take out my own money,' Madge told her. 'But Des said I could take out a bank loan if I wish.'

'Ah, Madge . . .' Harold was standing in the doorway. 'I thought I heard your voice.'

'Harold.' Madge looked momentarily flustered. 'I didn't know you were here.'

'I'm sorry,' Harold said, advancing into the room, 'but I couldn't help overhearing. Is it . . . are you . . . by any chance . . . are you having . . . ah . . . financial problems?'

'No,' Madge replied with a quick shake of her head. 'No, not really.'

'I wouldn't mind helping out if you were.'

Madge looked at him for a long moment. 'Well, yes,' she said at last. 'It's just that Henry has accumulated a few gambling debts which have to be paid off by tomorrow. If they are not, he could be in danger.'

'That's dreadful.' Harold clicked his tongue in disapproval. 'Is he asking you for the money?'

'Yes. I wasn't going to give it to him at first, but then when I saw what they had done to him . . .'

Charlene had been following this exchange with growing eagerness. 'You think Mum should help him out, don't you?' she asked Harold.

'Well . . .' Harold shifted uncomfortably and Charlene's hopes dipped a little. 'I think there's only one course of action you can take, Madge,' he said, 'and that is to make him stand on his own two feet.'

Charlene's hopes had now plummeted fully and shattered. She was stunned. She stared at Harold. 'What?'

'He has made his own bed, it seems to me,' Harold remarked.

Charlene was appalled. 'But he'll be killed.'

'Surely that's an exaggeration,' Harold said with a faint smile. 'From what I have heard of Henry, I am sure he can look after himself.'

'But you said . . .' She felt betrayed. She had been pinning her hopes on Harold who had seemed so sympathetic at the beginning. 'I'm glad you're not *my* father,' she cried, running from the room with tears in her eyes.

She hardly slept that night, worrying about what would happen to Henry as a result of her mother's callousness as she saw it. They were supposed to be picking him up this morning—but in what condition? Walking, or in a box? In the morning, she dressed very soberly in a black skirt and sweater. 'Couldn't you wear something brighter?' Madge asked her as she came into the kitchen. 'You look as though you're going to a funeral.'

'I probably am,' Charlene said glumly.

Madge was dressed and ready to go. 'Don't be ridiculous,' she snorted. 'Nothing's going to happen to Henry. Now you go and get changed. We don't want to be late for the bank.'

The bank? Charlene stared at her mother in surprise which gave way to delight as she finally grasped the significance of her words. 'Are you taking out the loan then?'

'If I can't get my hands on my own money,' Madge replied, 'I suppose I shall have to.'

With a joyous whoop, Charlene flung her arms around her mother and gave her a tight hug. 'Oh, Mum, I knew you would come through,' she laughed.

Gently, Madge disengaged herself from Charlene's embrace. 'Charlene . . .'

'I love you, Mum.'

'Charlene, I want you to understand that this is the last time ever that I shall help Henry.'

Charlene didn't believe it for a moment. 'It's the last time you'll have to, Mum—you'll see.'

Madge nodded to the door. 'Now go on. Get changed. We'll have to get the money to Henry.

Charlene frowned at her. 'But, Mum, you just can't walk

into the prison with a pile of cash and say, "Here you are." '

'Then what am I supposed to do with it?'

'Henry's got it all arranged.'

Madge nodded grimly. 'I should have realised that.'

When she had visited him, Henry had given his instructions very quietly, but distinctly. The money was to be handed to a woman who would be waiting for them in the car park behind Lassiter's Hotel at ten o'clock that morning. As soon as she had the money, this woman would pass the word to Henry's creditors in prison. Henry had explained it all very carefully. Madge was shocked when Charlene explained this arrangement. 'Do you mean to say that I have to hand over my hard-earned cash to some woman I've never seen before in my life?' she demanded.

'That's the idea.'

'But what guarantee do I have that she isn't a friend of Henry's . . . that they cooked up this scheme between them?'

'Henry wouldn't do that, Mum,' Charlene said emphatically. 'You know that.'

Madge sighed wearily and shook her head. 'I don't know anything any more,' she murmured.

'I'll give her the money if you like,' Charlene offered.

'No, I'll do it,' Madge said firmly. 'We'll go together.'

'Great.' Charlene smiled in satisfaction at this pleasing outcome. 'Then we'll go and pick up Henry. In one piece.'

'No, we won't,' Madge said flatly. 'If he's so clever at organising things, he can find his own way here.'

'But, Mum . . .'

'That's enough, Charlene. Now you go and get changed. We have to get to the bank . . .'

At the bank, there were forms to be filled in and signed. They were there for quite some time. Then they had to get to the car park behind Lassiter's Hotel where the woman contact, rather brassy and offhand, was waiting for them. Charlene knew her mother was disgusted and humiliated by the whole business; she wasn't feeling too happy about it herself. 'Come on, Charlene,' Madge said after the money had been handed over and the woman had gone. 'Let's go home.'

Charlene caught up with her mother who was walking briskly away from her. 'I know you said you didn't want to pick up Henry. But it would make me really happy if you did.'

Madge swung on her. 'That's all you care about, isn't it?' she accused angrily. 'Making Henry happy. Well, I'll tell you something, Charlene. I don't think I'll ever forgive you for what you've put me through. Either of you.'

Charlene stared miserably after her mother as she turned again and walked away from her.

Back at the house, waiting for Henry to arrive, the atmosphere was tense. Madge was in the kitchen, preparing lunch. Shane was reading the morning newspaper. 'Why don't you make yourself useful,' he said to Charlene, 'and help your Mum in the kitchen?'

Charlene didn't need any aggression from him. 'Why don't you go to work,' she snapped, 'instead of hanging around here and being a pain?' She sighed as Shane returned to his paper with a shrug. 'You'd think Mum would be pleased he's getting out,' she remarked with a puzzled glance in the direction of the kitchen.

Shane glared up at her from his paper. 'Sometimes I wonder what you have for a brain, Charlene,' he said in disgust. 'She was completely humiliated. She's been hurt. If I had known what you and Henry were scheming, I would have done the job myself.'

'Well, it's done now.' There was a knock at the front door. Charlene leapt excitedly to her feet. 'Mum, he's here,' she called into the kitchen as she ran along the hall to open the door.

Yes, and there he was—Henry with his wild hair and looking a little pale; with a tentative smile that broadened when he saw Charlene. 'Henry,' she cried, flinging herself at him, hugging him tightly.

'Ouch.' Henry winced and gently eased her away. 'The ribs, Lennie. Got to be careful.'

'Sorry.' In the excitement of seeing him again, Charlene had forgotten about his bruised ribs. She took his hand. 'Come in.' She led him into the living room where Shane

58

and Madge were looking a little ill at ease. 'Well?' Charlene challenged them when they remained silent. 'Someone could at least say something.'

'Hello, Henry,' Madge said stiffly.

'G'day, Mum.' He nodded to Shane. 'Shane.'

With a curt nod in return, Shane moved to the door. 'I have to go to work,' he said pointedly to Madge.

'Yes, all right.'

'It's great to be home, Mum.' Henry moved across the room to embrace his mother who remained quite rigid in his arms. 'And I promise I'll pay back every cent of that thousand dollars.'

Madge pushed him away. 'I'm sure you will,' she said coldly.

'Honestly, Mum,' Henry said with fervour. 'I've really learned my lesson this time. You'll never have to bail me out again.'

Madge drew herself up; she was looking very serious. 'Henry, I'm glad you're free,' she told him. 'And . . . I wish you the best for whatever you decide to do with your life.'

Henry and Charlene exchanged a puzzled glance. 'Oh come on, Mum,' Henry said with a nervous laugh. 'Let's be friends again.'

But Madge's expression remained stony. 'But I think you had better be on your way.'

Charlene was shocked; she had never seen her mother so coldly implacable. 'What are you talking about, Mum?' she cried. 'Henry's going to live here. With us.'

'He can't.' Madge shook her head. 'I'm sorry, Henry, but you have to take responsibility for your own life from now on. I've washed my hands of you. For good.'

'But, Mum . . .' Henry looked stunned. 'You don't really mean that do you?'

'I mean it, Henry.'

Henry began to plead with her. 'Mum, I know I've let you down in the past, and everything. But that's all finished now. I'm going to make a *go* of my life.'

'Mmmm.' Madge looked at him disbelievingly.

'I am,' Henry insisted. 'You don't think I *want* to go back to gaol, do you? You don't know what it's like in there. I'd have to be crazy . . . And if I'm to keep out of there, I've got to learn to live normally again. I'm going to need help. From both of you.'

Charlene could tell her mother wasn't swayed by Henry's persuasiveness. 'As usual,' Madge said drily.

'Mum!' Charlene exclaimed.

'It's all right,' Henry said quickly. 'It's the money. I don't blame her for being angry about it.'

'It wasn't the money,' Madge told him. 'It was the humiliation.'

'I really am sorry, Mum,' Henry said unhappily. 'I know how much you hate gambling. But . . . well, it did pass the time; I just got caught up, that's all.' He sighed. 'I've learnt my lesson this time. I won't let you down again. And I'll keep my promise. I'll pay you back every cent.'

Madge still wasn't convinced. 'You'd better go, Henry,' Charlene said bitterly. 'I don't think she's going to change her mind this time.'

'Yeah . . . I guess I'd better.' Henry looked beaten, a young man who had taken all the knocks he could bear. 'If it was anyone else, I'd say it was kicking a man while he's down.' He gave a small, sad smile; he blinked away tears. 'But not you two. You've been . . . fantastic. I want you both to know that . . .' he gulped . . . 'whatever happens to me from now on, I'll always be grateful.'

A picture of utter dejection, his head bowed, he turned to the door. As he did so, he gave a little cough. Madge's expression softened a little. 'Henry?'

Henry turned back to face her. 'Yes, Mum?'

'Have you got a cold?'

Her resistance had been broken. The performance had been too much for that maternal instinct of hers, lurking never too deeply beneath the forbidding surface, to withstand. Henry had won her, as he had always won her in the past and no doubt would continue to do so. Charlene smiled proudly at the glorious con-man who was her brother.

Five

The sun beat down on him; the air around him shimmered and pulsed in the heat. There was little shade; the nearest trees were about fifty yards away, across the stony, uneven ground with its occasional clumps of dry, spiky grass. He had tried to drag himself towards the trees which would offer him more shade, but with every movement he made, the pain shot viciously through his leg, forcing him to clench his teeth tightly together to stop himself from screaming. The sweat stung his eyes, and he could taste the salt on his lips. His throat was dry, but he needed to conserve the water in his bottle for as long as possible.

The throbbing echoes of the car had long since died away. There was nothing now but silence. He strained his ears for any sound on the road above the embankment— but there was nothing, no sound at all to be heard. He wondered where Des was; surely, it shouldn't be taking him so long; the telephone box was only a few hundred yards up the road. Once he had called the ambulance and returned . . . It shouldn't have taken him more than ten, twenty minutes at the most.

Fighting grimly against the surging pain, Jim had used a broken branch he had found lying nearby and some gauze from his first aid kit to fashion a makeshift splint for his broken leg. It helped, but not much; the pain was still very intense. 'Come on, Des,' he muttered through chapped lips. 'Where the hell are you?'

How many minutes had it been since Des, attracted by the sound of Jim's whistle, had appeared over the top of the embankment? 'What the hell happened, mate?' he had cried when he had seen Jim lying at the foot of the embankment.

Jim had been very weak, his consciousness losing focus then sharpening slightly again as Des scrambled down the embankment to his side. 'They . . . ran me off the road,' he had gasped as the pain clawed savagely at him again. 'My leg . . . I think it's broken. Get some help, Des.'

'No way, mate.' Des had grimly shaken his head. 'I can't leave you like this. Now . . . let's have a look at this leg.' Jim had yelped with pain as Des had tried to ease his grotesquely twisted leg into a more comfortable position. 'It's going to need a splint, mate.'

'No time for that . . . Call an ambulance. The telephone box . . .'

Earlier—how much earlier?—when he had sprinted up to the telephone box, Jim had seen the broken glass on the road, and the two kids who were about to wreak more damage on it. He had stopped them, made them believe, as Des had come panting up the road behind him, that there were at least twenty other guys running along in their wake. It hadn't been true, and the two punks must have realised that. Minutes later, the car had roared up behind Jim, once again well ahead of Des who was out of sight beyond a bend in the road, and had swerved deliberately towards him as he had turned into the embankment to allow it plenty of room to pass. Then when, to his horror, he had seen what they were trying to do to him, he had jumped back over the embankment, falling heavily, his leg twisting beneath him. A few minutes later, before Jim had properly recovered his senses enough to reach for his pack and take out the whistle which was there for just such emergencies as this, Des had come running past the spot, unaware that Jim was lying in pain on the other side of the embankment.

'Okay. I'll be on my way.' After establishing that Jim had plenty of food and water, Des had scrambled back up the embankment and sprinted off to seek help. All Jim could do was wait. He didn't think he would need to wait as long as this. But how long *had* he been waiting for Des to return? He wasn't sure; he couldn't be sure. It seemed like hours but it could, in fact, be no more than minutes that had elapsed since Des had run off to fetch help. The pain in his leg was excruciating; he felt himself close to blacking out, and tried to force himself to remain conscious and aware. He took a sip of water, but it hardly eased the dryness in his throat. So . . . where *was* Des?

It had been a silly dare, really. Des had made some comment about Jim's age, had accused him of being out of condition—and Jim had risen to the challenge. There had always been something of a friendly rivalry between them; now they had decided to put it to the test. To Jim, a cross-country run had seemed like a good idea. Between them, and with the aid of a map, they had plotted out a route. Jim had traced a line with his forefinger.

'That's the Levings Track. Scott and I did that a couple of years ago. And it's got the right length.'

'No, Jim. That gives you an unfair advantage.'

'How do you mean?'

'Well, if you've been over it before, you'll know all the nooks . . .'

'Fair enough. Okay then, why don't you choose one.'

'What about this one?'

'It's a creek bed.'

'Ah . . . well, yes, I know that. I was just making it more of a challenge.'

Jim's finger had traced another line on the map. 'We could do the Whittaker Track. I haven't done that one.'

'Wait a minute, Jim. Isn't that where those Scouts got lost last year? They had to send a helicopter in after them.'

'They would have been fine if they had stuck to the track. But if it worries you, we could stick to the tar-sealed roads through the park.'

'Oh, I don't know, Jim . . . I was looking forward to getting off the beaten track. Still, if that's what you want . . .'

'No, no, off the beaten track is fine by me.'

'Well, perhaps, on second thoughts . . .'

'We'll stick to the roads.'

'Daphne would be happier if we did.'

'Okay . . . so now what are we looking at? About twenty kilometres?'

'Oh, at least.'

'We'll have to take some food, some water, and some basic first aid equipment.'

'What for?'

'In case something goes wrong, and we have to stay overnight.'

'Overnight?'

'Not that I'm saying that anything *will* go wrong. But if it does, we'll be prepared, won't we?'

'Of course nothing will go wrong.'

If there was something wrong with the telephone, if it was out of order, or Des couldn't get through for some reason or another, then the car wasn't very far away. In that case, it would take a little longer. Sweating profusely, his shirt and shorts sticking to his body, Jim listened intently for any sound on the road above him, but all he could hear was the distant chirping of crickets.

'Dad, Mike and I were thinking . . . well, Daphne might feel better about it if we came along to keep an eye on you.'

'No, Scott. Definitely not. Des is feeling insecure enough as it is. And he has never done a race like this before. So how is he going to feel if he has to pull out and you guys are watching him? No, there'll be no spectators—all right?'

He could still hear nothing. He groaned softly and wiped the sweat from his forehead with the back of his hand. 'Are you sure you two are not going secretly off on some fishing trip?' Daphne had asked.

'Just the bare essentials,' Jim had said, giving his pack which Helen had prepared for him a pat with his hand.

They had expected to be back by about six that evening. They had taken Des's car. 'I'll have the linament ready,' Helen had said drily.

'Wish us luck,' Des had called to Helen and Daphne as he started the car.

'Just come back in one piece,' Daphne had cried after them as they drove away.

The gripping pain, and the sweat that stung his eyes. The waiting . . . 'I haven't been this far from civilisation since Mum sent me to Scout camp when I was twelve,' Des had said when they got out of the car.

The bush had stretched around them for miles upon miles. 'Just follow the road,' Jim had told him, 'and you'll be fine.'

Des had brought some chocolate. He handed a couple of bars to Jim, who had overlooked chocolate when preparing a list of the items he would carry in his pack. 'Thanks, mate. I should have thought of that myself.'

'What? You mean it's all right? Really?'

'Chocolate is made of sugar, and sugar is energy. We'll be needing all we can get before the day's over.'

'Why are you trying to demoralise me before we even get started?'

'Just a precaution, mate. Just a precaution.' He had given Des one of the two whistles he had thought to bring along with him. 'And this is essential.'

'You're kidding.'

'How will I find you when you get lost?'

'Me? No chance, pal.'

'Well . . . if either of us gets lost?'

Jim had soon taken the lead. He felt fine, in tip-top condition. He had run steadily, conserving his energy, and had hardly felt the weight of the pack on his back. He had thought of Des, labouring along somewhere behind him, and smiled. Poor Des had been trapped into it, really; he obviously hadn't expected Jim to rise to the bait. But he had been crowing so much about his own condition, also tip-top, that he could hardly have backed out of it no matter how much he would have wished it.

His throat was parched; he took another sip of water. If he hadn't brought the whistles along, Des would never have found him. He would have kept running the twenty kilometres or so on a route that would eventually bring him back to the car, in the belief that Jim was still somewhere ahead of him. The whistles . . . he had told Des that they were an essential item. His head was spinning, everything seemed to be spinning . . . With a massive effort of will, he tried to keep himself from slipping . . . Any moment now, he would hear the sound of a car on the road above him, perhaps an ambulance siren in the distance . . . Des *must* have gotten through to them by now and was already on his way back . . .

The beaten-up old car had been standing by the side of the road; that was the first thing he had noticed as he rounded the bend. Then, beyond the car, he had seen the telephone box, and the two kids, one of them with a short iron bar, who were converging on it with deliberate intention. 'Hey!' he had yelled, sprinting up to them. 'You two!'

They had swung on him, startled at first, then seeing he was alone, with surly belligerence. 'Rack off, Grandad,' one of them had snarled.

Catching his breath, Jim had faced them squarely. 'I'm not standing here . . .' He had drawn the breath deeply into his lungs. 'Telephones are here for . . . for emergencies,' he had panted. 'Not for fools like you to smash up when the mood takes you.'

The kid with the iron bar had advanced on him menacingly. 'You'd better keep running if you know what's good for you,' he had growled.

'I'm not going to let you smash the telephone box.'

'How do you figure on stopping us?'

They had moved slowly, threateningly towards him, but he had stood his ground, bluffing it out as he tried not to show his apprehension. 'What's this then? That's how you guys get your kicks, is it? Ganging up on a bloke with an iron bar?'

The one with the iron bar had smirked at his companion. 'Not much else to do here on a Sunday morning, is there, mate?'

'Hey, here's another one,' the second youth had observed as Des came running round the bend in the road.

Des had pulled up beside Jim. 'What's going on here?'

Jim had been thinking quickly. 'How far behind are the others?'

'Huh?'

'The others. How far behind?'

'Oh . . . about thirty seconds.'

Jim had turned back to the two youths who were no longer looking so sure of themselves. 'Right. So do you want to take the two of us on, and . . . maybe twenty other guys who are about thirty seconds behind us?'

And that had done it. The kids had sworn at them as they retreated to their car, then with an agonised screech of the tyres, had driven off in the direction from which Jim and Des had come.

'Thanks, mate,' Jim had said after they were gone.

'What were they after? You or the phone box?'

'Both.'

'Well, I hate to say this, but it gave me a chance to catch up with you. What do we do now?'

'I guess we start even. I owe you that much.'

'Suits me.'

Des had fallen behind him again. Just as he had rounded another bend, and was out of Des's sight, Jim had heard the car roaring up the road behind him. He had veered to the side of the road. The noise of the engine had screamed in his ears. Glancing back over his shoulder, he had seen the car, the same beaten-up model with scratches and dints, and a cracked headlight, that had been parked beside the telephone box, hurtling towards him. Just before he jumped over the embankment, he had caught a glimpse of the leering faces of the two youths who had advanced on him so menacingly when he had stepped in to stop them vandalising the telephone box.

'Jim! Jim!' The voice seemed to have no definition, as if it were coming from a vast, echoing distance. 'Jim, it's me!'

Battling against the fierce pain in his leg, Jim forced himself to open his eyes and concentrate on the figure that was towering above him. Slowly, indistinctly, he recognised Des. 'When are they coming, mate?' he whispered.

'Sorry, mate.' Des shook his head gloomily. 'Those rotten mongrels . . . they tore the phone apart. They must have gone straight back.'

'The car?' There was still the car.

'They got to that as well,' Des bitterly informed him. 'Let the air out of the tyres, ripped out the wiring, took the distributor cap. Thought I'd better come back here. There was nothing I could do.' His face shiny with perspiration, he was panting heavily. With an effort, Jim reached for his pack. 'Hey, take it easy, mate.'

After rummaging for a few moments, Jim found the map and managed to open it out. Finding the spot in the national park where he estimated them to be, he pointed to it with a shaking finger. 'Here . . . look,' he said with difficulty as Des squatted down beside him. 'You'll have to . . .' His finger moved across the map. 'There's the main road. About ten kilometres . . .'

'And the rest.' Des was peering closely at the map. 'It's all through bush.'

'But it's thirty kilometres by road.' He stared beseechingly up at Des, only dimly discerning his worried expression. He didn't know how much longer he could stand the pain. 'Please, Des. Please hurry.'

Des pushed himself up onto his feet. 'Right.' Reaching forward, he eased Jim's pack under his head as a pillow. 'Just take it easy. I'll be as quick as I can.'

'Yeah . . .' Jim's head slumped back onto the makeshift pillow.

He had fallen heavily, his leg buckling beneath him. There had been the intense, rocketing pain, and he had lain there, struggling to catch his breath as the car that had almost killed him had sped off down the road. He had heard its engine, loud at first, then diminishing as the distance between them increased. The sound of that engine had hovered in the air for a long time afterwards. He had thought it had eventually faded into the silence which he recalled vaguely as having been particularly intense; he remembered having strained to hear any sound at all on the road above. But he must have been mistaken; he could still hear it after all, a distant throbbing in the air. His eyes jerked open; he listened carefully. Yes, there it was, quite distinct—but instead of fading away, as he had thought, it was coming closer. A car—definitely a car. Suddenly, he was very alert; all the fuzziness had gone, fragmented thoughts of cars going and cars coming. What remained—and most vividly—was the knowledge that a car was coming along the road towards him.

It was a chance. It would take ages for Des to reach the main road through the bush. He had to make the effort to reach the road in the hope of flagging down the approaching car. The situation was desperate. There wasn't much time; a couple of minutes, that was all.

Rolling over, and with his broken leg sticking out a slight angle from his body, careful not to put any more pressure on it than was absolutely essential, he brought up his good knee which, with his hands pressing hard on the ground, he used as a lever to push himself upright. With the sweat streaming from him, gasping and wincing from the pain, he managed to get up onto his good leg, then hopping a couple of paces, staggering and almost falling, flung himself at the embankment.

His fingers scrabbling in the dirt, he clawed his way up the embankment. Dislodged stones rolled away from beneath him. The pain the huge effort was causing him was unbearable. His breath came in ragged gasps; the streaming sweat blinded him as he dragged himself up, inch by agonising inch. Suddenly, when he was almost at the top of the embankment, he realised with sickening dismay that he had left his whistle behind. The car was coming rapidly closer.

Summoning the little that remained of his strength, he threw himself to the top of the embankment just as the car, barely more than a flash of green, sped past him. 'Help,' Jim called out in weak desperation—but it was no use; the car was too far away.

And then the pain struck him with more force than ever. With a tortured cry, he clasped his leg and rolled over onto his side as everything started spinning again, as the world lurched, trees whirled and toppled, and the sky became steadily darker . . .

How long had he been unconscious? There was no way of knowing. All he knew was that someone was holding his wrist. His eyes fluttered open. He blinked at the dark figure that was squatting beside him. 'You'll be all right,' a voice said. 'I'll radio for an ambulance.'

'What . . . ?'

'I saw the car back there along the road. I thought something might be wrong.'

He could see more clearly now. A pale blue shirt, polished leather, sunlight glinting on a silver badge—and behind the policeman, a powerful and gleaming motorbike resting on its stand at the side of the road. It was gradually coming back to him—the desperate climb up the embankment, the car disappearing around the bend in the road, the pain . . .

'Good old Des.' His voice was barely more than a croak. He smiled weakly. 'I knew he would get through.'

'Des? Who's Des?'

'We were running together. He went to get help.' Seeing the uncomprehending expression on the young patrolman's face, he struggled up into a sitting position. The pain lanced him, but not so sharply as before. 'He's all right, isn't he?'

'I don't know, sir. I haven't seen your friend.' Straightening, the patrolman moved quickly across to his motorbike. 'I'll call the ambulance now,' he said, picking up the handset of his radio while Jim stared at him in mounting alarm. 'I'll also ask if anybody knows anything about your friend.'

The next few hours passed as if in a daze. Only dimly was he aware of the ride back in the ambulance, of being lifted on a stretcher while people said reassuring things to him that he didn't understand. He was conscious of looming whitewashed walls and that compounded smell that he always associated with hospitals. He heard footsteps echoing in corridors. Nurses came and went, and he was given something to ease the pain. A doctor told him that his leg was broken and that he was suffering from a mild case of exposure—but otherwise he was all right; he would be able to go home in the morning after his leg had been set. He slept a little, then woke up to find Helen sitting anxiously beside his bed. 'Have they found Des?'

Helen shook her head. 'They'll keep searching as long as there's enough light.'

'And Daphne?' She would be absolutely frantic.

'I'm going there now.'

It was a long and anxious night. It was almost impossible not to believe that the worst had not happened to Des, particularly when it was realised, on consulting the map, just how rough that country was. Then, when it was seen that Des would have to cross a creek where there were apparently only a couple of places easy enough to ford without having to swim across, and Daphne had given a cry of dismay and said that Des hated water and could hardly swim, the odds against his survival rose considerably. Perhaps he hadn't attempted to cross the creek, Helen had suggested without real hope, and turned back. But Daphne had dismissed this. Knowing Jim was badly hurt and counting on him, he would have tried to get across somehow.

But then, in the morning, to everybody's huge relief, the good news came through. Des had been found. He had spent the night on a rock after having tried to swim the creek which he described some time later, after he had been brought back home from the hospital where he had spent some time under observation, as a raging torrent. 'I was lucky enough to find a rock stuck out in the middle. Once I had got out of the water, there was no way I was going to get back in again. And it got dark . . . and that was it. Took me till morning to pluck up the courage to risk it.'

Jim came home on a pair of crutches and with his leg in plaster. He was still not used to the crutches, and was a little unsteady. Helen tried to fuss over him, but he brushed her aside. Even if the doctor had said that he needed lots of rest, it didn't mean that she had to mollycoddle him.

'Whether you like it or not,' Helen said sternly, 'your body has undergone a lot of punishment. The trouble is, you don't realise that.'

'But that doesn't mean to say I have to be some sort of an outlet for your infernal maternal instincts,' Jim said with mock gruffness, as he manoeuvred himself on the crutches across to the sofa and with a little difficulty eased himself onto it.

'Oh . . .' Helen regarded him with mild exasperation. 'You and Des can thank your lucky stars that you came out of this little escapade without more damage being done.'

'I know.' Even the good news, broken to him by Helen in the hospital, that Des had been found had not done much to assuage his feelings of guilt. 'And if it hadn't been for me, Des wouldn't have been in an escapade at all. Daphne would have been spared all the worry.'

'Well, you're both home now,' Helen said with a gentle smile. 'And that's the way Daphne and I would like it to stay.' She waggled a reproving finger at him. 'And no more talk of long distance runs . . . at least until you've recovered from the last one.'

Six

There was a lot to do; so much that needed to be sorted out. Helen was in a flurry and close to panic. What with one thing and another, it had completely slipped her mind that she was having an exhibition of her paintings next month.

The director of the gallery had just called and asked her when she would be taking the pictures in for the exhibition, and she had fibbed a little, telling him that she had almost completed going through her catalogue when, in fact, surrounded by absolute chaos, hardly anything at all had been done. And then there was all that stuff in the garage which hadn't been touched at all. Half of it at least still needed to be framed. She didn't know how she was going to manage.

Jim helped her divide the paintings in the garage into two separate boxes—one for the paintings she intended to exhibit, the other for the rejects which she would eventually paint over. When that was done, a third pile remained. These were the undecideds, which after thinking about it for a few minutes, Helen nominated for the box containing the exhibition paintings. She would sift them all again before making her final selection. So that she would know which box contained which, she asked Jim to place the box of good paintings to the right, and the rejects to the left.

When young Henry Mitchell from next door, who had been showing more than a passing interest in the clearing activities in the Robinson garage, learned from Scott that Helen had no further use for some of her paintings, he had an idea. Why, instead of throwing them out or whatever, couldn't he try and sell them for her? It was crazy to throw out things like that when there was the possibility of money to be made. He had seen the paintings and some of them were very good, in his opinion. People paid big money, he said, for stuff that was much worse. He was sure he could get rid of a few of them by taking them from door to door.

'Do you really think so?' Helen asked him.

'I'd like to give it a try.'

Helen was interested. She had always been a perfectionist as far as her art was concerned, and if it hadn't gone right, even to the extent of a brushstroke, she was in the habit of discarding a painting without any further thought. But if Henry could sell them . . . 'We can go halves,' she said. 'Is that fair enough?' She would be happy enough to cover the cost of the canvas.

'You bet.' Henry grinned at her.

'They're in the garage,' she told him. 'The box on the left. Don't touch the box on the right under any circumstances.'

'Got it, Mrs Daniels,' Henry said cheerfully.

She didn't realise anything was wrong until that evening when she sent Scott to the garage to bring in the box containing the good paintings. Mrs Mangel had just been on the phone to Jim, enquiring about some paintings that Henry Mitchell was trying to sell her. She had been suspicious, it seemed; apparently she had thought that Henry might have stolen them. Jim had assured her that it was all right, that Helen had given Henry permission to sell the paintings.

When Scott brought the box of paintings into the house from the garage, Helen began to go through them with the purpose of sifting out the ones she wanted for her exhibition. She turned over one painting, then another. She was puzzled. Surely these were not the ones she had put aside for further consideration. She flicked over some more of the paintings. They were definitely not the ones. In rising panic, she hurried into the kitchen where Jim and Scott had begun to serve out dinner. 'Scott, is there another box of paintings in the garage?'

'No.' With a puzzled frown, Scott shook his head. 'Henry took the other box.'

Then that meant . . . 'He's taken the wrong one,' Helen cried in alarm. 'The ones you brought in are the rejects.'

'Gran, that's all there was,' Scott insisted. 'It's not my fault. Someone else must have taken them.'

'Ah . . .' Jim's expression had become suddenly bleak. 'I did.'

'What?' Helen stared at him in dismay.

'I wasn't thinking,' Jim murmured unhappily. 'I had to move the box when I put the car away. It was in the way.'

Helen was aghast at what this meant. If Henry had taken the wrong box . . . 'Then he's got all my paintings for the exhibition,' she moaned in desperation. 'Thousands of dollars' worth.'

Jim was looking very miserable at the recollection of what he had done in an unthinking moment. 'We just have to pray that he hasn't sold any yet,' he said glumly, and Helen shuddered at the thought that it might already be too late.

And it was, as she discovered in horror some minutes later when, after recalling Mrs Mangel's telephone call, she had run across the street to her house. 'Yes, of course I bought one of your paintings,' Mrs Mangel said rather importantly as she led Helen into the living room. 'Being a well known patron of the arts, I decided to ignore the expense.'

And there it was, the painting, propped up against the wall—and of all the paintings Mrs Mangel could have brought as a local patron of the arts, this one, of the church where Helen and Bill had been married all those years ago, was the prize of the bunch. Not only did it have great sentimental value for Helen, but she had thought, if she was lucky, she might be able to sell it for as much as eight hundred dollars. With a proud smile, Mrs Mangel picked up the painting.

'I found a lovely old frame in the shed which would suit it nicely,' she said. 'But I'm afraid it doesn't quite fit. So . . . I thought I would have to chop the painting a little. Here . . .' her hand moved vertically down one side of the canvas, lopping off about one third of a weeping willow tree, then with a horizontal sweep obliterating a sizeable section of sky and fluffy cloud . . . 'and there. It will fit the frame perfectly then.'

With an anguished cry, Helen seized the painting from her. 'You'll do no such thing,' she exclaimed. 'Don't you *dare* touch it.'

'Mrs Daniels . . .' Mrs Mangel was taken aback. 'Please . . . please control yourself.' She drew herself up in offended dignity. 'Really! I'm surprised. I bought that painting, It's mine—and I'll do what I like with it.'

Helen was clutching the painting tightly against her. She shook her head. Jim came running into the room. 'Thank God I've found you,' he said in breathless relief. 'Come on,' he urged Helen. 'Henry has the whole box of paintings down at the coffee shop.'

'But . . .' Helen stared at him helplessly. 'Nell has the painting of the church.'

'Mrs Mangel can wait,' Jim said as Mrs Mangel snatched the painting back from Helen.

Helen glared ferociously at Mrs Mangel. 'I'll be back,' she warned. 'And if you do take the scissors to the painting . . .' her pointing finger almost touched Mrs Mangel's nose . . . 'I'll take them to you.'

With a gasp, her eyes wide with shock, Mrs Mangel recoiled. Jim hustled Helen out of the house.

'Well, what do you know,' Henry said cheerfully as they hurried into the coffee shop some minutes later. 'Just the woman I wanted to see.' With a sinking sensation, Helen noted how pleased with himself he seemed.

Jim bore down on him. 'Henry, have you sold any more of those paintings?' he demanded.

'Any more?' Henry grinned conspiratorially at Mike Young who was working behind the counter. 'Did you hear that, Mike? Have I sold any more of the paintings?' He turned back to Jim with a broad smile. 'You happen to be looking at the salesman of the year,' he said proudly, tapping himself on the chest. 'I got rid of the lot.' Helen sank weakly onto a chair. 'Actually, you've only just missed the blokes who bought them.'

'Really!' Jim and Helen exchanged a stricken glance. 'How much did they pay for them?'

'Six hundred and eighty big ones, all up,' Henry replied. 'Isn't that terrific?'

'Just fabulous, Henry,' Helen said dismally. 'Just fabulous.' She sighed and looked up at Jim. 'Well, I don't have to worry any more, do I? No pictures . . . no exhibition.'

She was a little calmer by the time she returned to Mrs Mangel's house; she was determined to be quite reasonable. 'You don't still intend to damage my painting?' she asked.

Mrs Mangel had greeted her coldly. 'That depends on one's interpretation of the word "damage", doesn't it? Its present size makes it a little . . . unwieldy.'

'Nell, if I could just explain . . .'

'And possession *is* nine tenths of the law, as they say.'

It was a struggle for Helen to show restraint. 'All right, then,' she said shortly. 'Gloves off. I won't waste your time, and I trust you won't waste mine. That painting is profoundly important to my exhibition.' She opened her purse. 'There's been a misunderstanding, and I'll be happy to reimburse you.' She fished inside her purse. 'You paid thirty dollars, I believe.'

'That's correct,' Mrs Mangel said stiffly.

Helen held the money out to her. 'I'd like to think that the matter has now been resolved,' she said.

But Mrs Mangel ignored the money Helen was holding out to her. 'It's a lovely painting,' she said with a firm shake of her head. 'A little on the bulky side perhaps, but that could simply be personal taste . . .'

'Nell, this isn't a game.' Helen was becoming thoroughly exasperated with this woman's obstinacy. 'Without that painting, I can't have that exhibition.'

Mrs Mangel allowed herself a small smile. 'Well, that's your problem, isn't it? I'm not sure I even I want to sell it now.'

Seeing that she was unable to budge the woman, Helen stormed back to her own house. She was in a fury, ready to explode. 'Don't explode,' Jim said quietly as he manoeuvred her to a chair. 'Just sit.'

'I was courteous, I was patient . . .' She shook her head helplessly. 'That woman is unbelievable.'

'I take it she refused.'

Helen glowered at him; the last thing she needed to have stated to her right now was the obvious. 'She almost looked as if she was enjoying herself. If . . . if she so much as touches that painting . . .' She groaned. 'I'll have to cancel the exhibition.'

'Oh, Helen . . .'

'Well? Do you have any other bright ideas?' Of course he didn't. 'It's going to be a monumental non-event now,' she said miserably. She sighed. 'Twenty-five picture hooks and some ordinary wallpaper.'

'Well, at least it will be different.'

'I need a brandy.' Helen shuddered. 'Oh . . . that . . . *woman!*'

Apart from Mrs Mangel, Henry had sold the paintings to two men who had thought they could easily sell them for a profit in the United States where Australian works of art were having a successful run at the moment. They had paid for them by cheque. Learning from Henry that these men were staying at Lassiter's Hotel, Jim, still guilt-ridden by the knowledge that it had been his fault that the mix-up had occurred in the first place, offered to try and get them back. He was sure they would be reasonable about it after he had explained the situation to them. He came back with some good news. He had managed to buy back the paintings.

'How much?' Helen asked.

'Just what they paid for them. We joggers can be down-right reasonable when it comes down to it, you know.'

Helen was delighted. 'How on earth did you manage that? What did you tell them?'

Jim shrugged offhandedly. 'It turns out that they're heading for the States in a couple of days,' he said, 'and they need some contacts for their manufacturing business.'

'And so you were able to help them.'

'They were most appreciative.'

'And they sold the paintings back to you for six hundred and fifty dollars?'

'I returned the cheque,' Jim said with a nod. 'Plus a little extra for their trouble.'

'Oh Jim, I could kiss you,' Helen cried happily. 'In fact, I will.' She kissed him and gave him an ecstatic hug.

'That just leaves one small stumbling block,' Jim observed.

Oh yes. Mrs Mangel. 'I was just on my way there.'

'I'll come with you.'

Mrs Mangel was all sweetness and light as she let them into the house. 'This is a social visit, I take it. How nice.'

'You know why we're here, Nell,' Helen said crisply.

'The painting?' Mrs Mangel dismissed this with a wave of her hand. 'Oh, that's too trifling to worry about, surely.'

Once again, Helen was finding it difficult to summon the necessary patience with this infuriating woman. 'Trifling to you, perhaps,' she said evenly. 'But certainly not to me. Look, Nell, I'm asking you again, please reconsider . . .'

Mrs Mangel seemed to be enjoying Helen's dilemma. There was a sly look in her eyes. 'Well, I *could* sell it back, I suppose. But I do wish you had been honest with me in the first place. Perhaps if you had told me that it was so valuable, the decision might have been easier.'

Suddenly sensing pitfalls ahead of her, Helen chose her words carefully. 'Nell, that painting is very valuable to me.'

'And very important to the exhibition,' Jim added.

'Yes, I know.' Mrs Mangel smiled in a way that was worrying to Helen. 'Important, certainly. To the extent of eight hundred dollars, I believe.'

Helen's mouth fell open. 'Who told you that?'

'Henry Mitchell,' Mrs Mangel replied. 'He was concerned about how much insurance I might have to pay.'

Helen was appalled that Henry, no matter how innocently, had let slip the fact, and to this woman in particular, that she believed the painting of the church to be worth eight hundred dollars at least. She had been so upset with Henry when she learned he had sold her paintings that she

had come right out with it and told him that the one he
had sold to Mrs Mangel alone was worth so much. Henry
had tried to make amends; he had offered to use a little
persuasion on Mrs Mangel to give up the painting, but
Helen had told him sharply not to interfere or she would
come down on him like a ton of bricks. Hadn't he already
done enough? Between his gentle persuasion and Jim's
considerable talent at rearranging the garage, Helen's exhibition now had every chance of being a five-star disaster.
She thought she had made the message abundantly clear,
but Henry had gone ahead, anyway—and now, as a result,
the situation had been made drastically worse.

'But we can't possibly pay that much.'

'Oh . . .' Mrs Mangel looked offended. 'Nor would I ask
you to pay so much,' she said loftily. 'After all, we *are*
neighbours. No, in all conscience, the most I could ask
would be six hundred.'

'Six hundred!' Shocked, Helen glanced at Jim who was
looking quite woebegone.

Mrs Mangel's smile was quite condescending. 'I've grown
very attached to it,' she said. 'It's not an easy decision for
me to have to make, you know.'

But Jim had already made his own decision. 'I'll get my
chequebook.'

'No, Jim.' Helen grabbed his arm as he turned to leave.
It was completely out of the question. 'I will not be held
to ransom in this way.' She swung angrily back to face Mrs
Mangel. 'All right then,' she cried. 'You're welcome to the
painting. You can desecrate it, mutilate it, chop it up into
tiny pieces and send them out as Christmas cards, if you
like. But I have no intention of paying you one red cent.
Come on, Jim,' she commanded as she turned again to
sweep furiously out of the house of the woman who had
just proved that she was nothing more than a common
blackmailer.

When Mrs Mangel had a sudden change of heart, Helen
was at first astonished, then delighted—and was quite prepared to acknowledge that she wasn't such a bad stick after
all. What prompted this change of heart, she could only

surmise. Perhaps it was Jane, her grand-daughter, who had made her see reason—or enough of it to set the workings of her conscience in motion. Anyway, here she was, at the front door with the painting under her arm. 'I've been thinking, Mrs Daniels,' she said uncomfortably. 'Perhaps I wasn't being fair. As you said, a misunderstanding . . . Of course, I shall need my thirty dollars back.'

'Of course. Please come in.' .

Helen led her into the living room which was strewn with the paintings she had selected for her exhibition. 'Believe me, it's not an easy thing to do.'

'I'm sure.'

Mrs Mangel stared gloomily at Helen's paintings. 'It just seemed so right for my living room . . . if you know what I mean.'

Helen nodded. 'An unfortunate misunderstanding.'

'I gave it a lot of thought, Mrs Daniels.'

'I'm sure you did.'

'It just wouldn't have been right. An unfair advantage, you might say.' Still clutching Helen's painting, Mrs Mangel abruptly changed the subject. 'I notice there are no portraits here,' she observed.

'No.'

'What a pity,' Mrs Mangel said distantly. 'Do you know, it has always been the greatest ambition of mine to find an artist who would be kind enough to . . .' She smiled wanly, then with a sigh, shook her head. 'Well, we can all dream, can't we?'

Helen tried to sidestep what she recognised as a blatant hint, a classic case of tit-for-tat. She laughed a little uncertainly. 'Well . . . yes . . . it's a very specialised art form. I'm afraid I have only dabbled . . .'

'Oh, what am I doing?' Mrs Mangel suddenly seemed surprised to realise that she was still holding onto Helen's painting. She offered it to Helen. 'Here you are, Mrs Daniels,' she said with a small and enigmatic smile. 'From a . . . friend.'

Feeling trapped, Helen took the painting. 'Perhaps, when the exhibition is over . . .' She managed a tight smile.

'Perhaps I could try to do your portrait. But I can't guarantee anything, though.'

'What a lovely gesture.' Mrs Mangel beamed at her. 'Oh . . . and now I believe there's a small matter of thirty dollars . . .'

Helen had her painting back, and that was the main thing. She didn't really mind the fact that she had been conned at the same time into painting Mrs Mangel's portrait. As she told Scott when he queried why she had allowed herself to be talked into it, she was a pushover, as soft as marshmallow, that was her. In the meantime, she began to prepare some preliminary sketches for the portrait. If she could finish it in time, she might include it in the exhibition.

'Do you think it might give you a better chance of impressing the critics?' Mrs Mangel asked when Helen suggested this to her.

'You never know,' Helen replied. 'And it *would* show a different facet of my work. But we shall have to begin immediately.'

'Yes, of course, Mrs Daniels.' Mrs Mangel was obviously delighted with the prospect of having her portrait included in Helen's exhibition. 'Just let me know when you are ready.'

Because Mrs Mangel was a restless woman who fidgeted a great deal, Helen didn't find the going particularly easy—but she persevered, working quickly and deftly to portray the seated figure in front of her on the canvas. She refused to allow her subject to see the work before it was finished, which irked Mrs Mangel. 'It's very frustrating, I must say,' she complained, 'not knowing what's going on behind there.'

'You'll just have to wait, Nell,' Helen told her. 'It won't be long now.'

She was pleased with the way the portrait was working out. 'Surely you can't stop me seeing it now,' Mrs Mangel said peevishly when Helen announced that it was virtually finished.

'When it's framed,' Helen said as she covered the canvas with a sheet.

The time was fast running out. Besides the frame for Mrs Mangel's portrait, there were still the other paintings to be catalogued and taken to the gallery for hanging. Helen was working very hard; it was important to her that the exhibition be a success. It became even more so when she received a telegram from Gerard Singer in America, informing her that his new agent, one Chris Wilton, who was in the country in search of new and promising talent, had shown an interest in viewing Helen's exhibition.

If Helen was pleased with Mrs Mangel's portrait, the subject herself, on the other hand, was far from pleased when she finally saw it on the day the exhibition was to open. Chocking back a scream, she pronounced it hideous. Helen tried to calm her. 'It's a *painting*, not a photograph.'

'It's a monstrosity.' With one hand to her throat, Mrs Mangel stared at the portrait with wide, horrified eyes. 'I've never been so insulted in my life.'

Helen tried to explain. 'Artists are *supposed* to go beyond actual appearances,' she pointed out. 'I've used . . . well, we call it artistic licence, because I wanted to capture your essential character. It's the way I really see you.' She glanced at the angularities and vivid sworls of the portrait. Yes, it *was* the way she had seen her subject; she thought she had captured the essential quality very well.

'*Artistic!*' Mrs Mangel snorted angrily. 'I wonder that you *dare* use the word. And if *that* is how you see me. . . .' her finger jabbed in agitation towards the cause of her outrage . . . 'I suggest you need new glasses—and the sooner the better.'

Helen was still trying to appease her. 'I daresay you were expecting a more . . . conventional approach. But I wanted to try a new style. I think I might have explained that to you at the beginning.'

'I don't know *what* you explained, but that . . . that . . .' Once more Mrs Mangel's quivering finger pointed at the offending portrait. 'It's nothing more than a . . . caricature.' She shook her head in woeful self-reproach. 'I should never have agreed to sit for you.'

'I wish you wouldn't take it so personally,' Helen said. 'You see . . .' She indicated the canvas. 'I have concentrated on depth and texture, and . . . well, yes, just a slight exaggeration. But that's only to bring out the person behind the image. Actually, I think it looks rather regal.'

'Regal . . . ?' Mrs Mangel looked momentarily confused, then her voice hardened again. 'No, I won't allow it to go on public display,' she snapped. 'Under no circumstances.'

'But, Nell, you know it's not meant . . .'

'You're wasting your breath, Mrs Daniels.' Striding across to the portrait, Mrs Mangel snatched it up. 'I'm taking this . . . this thing with me before anyone else sees it. It will make excellent kindling for the barbecue.'

Moving quickly across to her, Helen stopped her by placing a firm hand on the frame of the painting. 'That portrait is part of my exhibition,' she said in a low, threatening tone, 'and that's exactly where it's going.'

Mrs Mangel tried to pull the painting away, but Helen was holding on to it too tightly. 'Over my dead body.'

'Don't tempt me.'

'I don't want anyone to see it—and that's final.'

'Oh, come on, Nell, you know it's just vanity . . .'

'It is *not* vanity,' Mrs Mangel retorted. 'It's self-preservation. No, Mrs Daniels, I will *not* be made a mockery of . . .'

'It's my painting,' Helen insisted. 'I can do what I like with it.'

'Oh no. You painted it for me. That makes it *my* property.'

'It will be. After the exhibition.'

'Now.'

'No.' This time, Helen managed to wrest the portrait from Mrs Mangel's grasp.

'Oh, very well,' Mrs Mangel said tautly and with a toss of her head as she headed for the door in high dudgeon. 'Have it your own way. But you'll be hearing from me. Legally. There are such things as injunctions, you know.'

After she had gone, Helen glumly contemplated the portrait she thought had come off rather well. Perhaps it was understandable that Mrs Mangel had been shocked by it, she conceded, but she hadn't expected her to react so savagely. But then she consoled herself with the added reflection that Mrs Mangel probably still would have complained however it had turned out, if it had been more flattering and not compounded of the sharpnesses and angles with which she had chosen to portray her subject, seeing in them the essential key to the woman's character. But perhaps the eyes *were* a little too yellow, the nose a little too long and sharp, the mouth too non-existent. And there was the adam's apple. And all that purple . . . Helen decided she was still pleased with the outcome. It was, she felt, quite spiritual.

She was a little surprised when the agent Gerard Singer had telegraphed her about from America turned out to be a woman. Chris Wilton—she had assumed . . . 'Oh yes, of course,' she said to the rather stylish young woman who was standing on the front porch, and who had just introduced herself as Christine Wilton, when enlightenment finally dawned. 'Gerard did send a telegram to say that you were coming.' She opened the door wider. 'Please come in,' she invited. 'I'm afraid it's all rather chaotic at the moment. There's so much to do. I didn't realise how nerve-wracking an exhibition can be.'

As she stepped into the hall, Chris Wilton laughed. 'I haven't yet met an artist who doesn't suffer from first night nerves,' she observed. 'But from what Gerard has told me of your work, I'm sure you have nothing to worry about.'

Helen closed the door behind them. 'I hope you're right,' she said without conviction, as the spectre of Mrs Mangel suddenly rose up in front of her.

Chris Wilton had brought with her the painting Helen had begun in New York and had left with Gerard who, while reluctant to part with it, had said it was too good to remain unfinished. The painting of the gently rolling countryside just outside the city revived bitter-sweet memories for Helen which she quickly suppressed. Chris was studying the portrait of Mrs Mangel. 'Is this your work, too?' she queried.

'It was an experiment, really,' Helen told her. 'I wanted to extend myself a little further.'

Putting on a pair of glasses, Chris examined the portrait more closely. 'Ah . . . so it seems . . . yes, a complete break in style for you. It's very good. Those fingers . . . so talon-like, so expressive . . . yes, powerful . . . and the nose . . .' She turned back to Helen. 'This will be part of your showing, naturally.'

'That was the plan, but unfortunately the subject has other ideas.'

Chris raised her eyebrows. 'You mean she doesn't like it?'

'I think that would be the understatement of the year,' Helen said with a wry smile.

'In that case, she has very little appreciation of art,' Chris remarked. 'But of course you'll exhibit it, anyway.'

'Well, it isn't as simple as that,' Helen told her. 'You see, I told her she could have the painting—so she does have a point. On top of which I wouldn't put it past her to make trouble this evening and ruin everything.'

'I see . . .' Chris was peering at the portrait again. 'Well, she does look quite severe at that . . . Too bad. It should be the focal point of your work.'

'It won't be, if she has her way.'

'And yet, you know,' Chris said thoughtfully, 'it does have the kind of strength you associate with the tough old girls who whipped their wagons across the prairies and tamed the Wild West. Except that she is Australian. So it would be your Outback instead of the American prairies. Perhaps you should call it . . . ah, let me see . . . yes, something along the lines of "The Pioneering Spirit." '

' "The Pioneering . . ."' Helen studied the painting with renewed interest; she hadn't quite seen it that light before. The Pioneering Spirit. Mrs Mangel. It was an intriguing thought.

Only a couple of hours before the exhibition was to open, Chris asked if she could photograph the portrait, as it was her intention to take photographs of any works that interested her while she was in the country so they could be assessed for their suitability for a collection of contemporary Australian art which she planned to put together on her return to New York. Helen readily agreed, although she did feel the need to point out that the gallery had a strict rule about photographs being taken on the premises. It was Jim, who had arrived home in the meantime, who suggested that Chris take the portrait back to her room at Lassiter's Hotel, photograph it there, then bring it along to the gallery afterwards. It wouldn't take more than a few minutes, and Lassiter's was on the way to the gallery. Chris thought that was a great idea. 'Well, in that case, we had better be going,' Helen said. The exhibition was opening at seven, and it was already after five.

With the portrait wrapped in a blanket, Helen and Chris were carrying it into the hotel when Henry Mitchell came up to them. 'Anything I can do?' he asked when he saw they were having a little trouble with it because of its awkward size.

'Oh, Henry.' Helen was pleased to see him. 'Just the person we need.' She nodded towards Chris. 'I'd like you to meet Chris Wilton.'

'We've already met,' Henry said with a grin.

'Oh?'

'He bought me a drink,' Chris explained. 'A total stranger. I thought it was very nice of him.' It seemed to Helen that the smile Chris directed back at Henry was just a fraction flirtatious, but she was much too worried about her exhibition to be more than just slightly intrigued by it.

'We'd better get this upstairs,' she said. 'Time's marching on. Do be careful, Henry.'

'I'll guard it with my life,' Henry promised. Chris had explained that they were taking the portrait to her room so she could photograph it.

While the photographs were being taken, Helen decided to wait with her grandson, Paul, who was working back in his office at the hotel. She was very nervous. 'Don't worry,'

Paul tried to reassure her. 'The exhibition will go like clockwork, and you'll be the toast of Erinsborough.'

They seemed to be taking a long time over the photographs. Helen clasped and unclasped her hands; she was very fidgety. 'That wouldn't be prejudice on your part, would it?'

'Of course not,' Paul replied earnestly. 'I think you've worked very hard—and tonight you will reap the rewards.'

Helen could only hope he was right. 'If only that Mangel woman doesn't put on one of her performances . . .'

'Don't worry about her. Now you just go and make yourself look beautiful.'

'All right then.' Helen stood up. 'But first I had better call Chris and see if she has finished with the portrait.'

But when she dialled the number of Chris's room, there was no reply. She let it ring for some minutes, but there was still no answer. 'That's odd,' she said with a puzzled frown as she replaced the receiver. 'She's not there.'

'Maybe she's in the shower,' Paul suggested.

'Yes . . . or perhaps she and Henry have taken the portrait back to the car.'

'Probably. Anyway, she knows you're running short on time.'

Helen was moving to the door when it suddenly opened and Mrs Mangel hurried in with a pile of towels. Helen drew back. 'No, Nell,' she said quickly. 'I've made my decision. You're not going to talk me out of it.'

But it seemed that in her role as the hotel's housekeeper, Mrs Mangel had other things on her mind. Ignoring Helen, she addressed Paul with an air of some importance. 'You'd better come with me, Mister Robinson. There seems to be an altercation in room 203.'

The number registered immediately with Helen; Chris had mentioned it either in the car or when Henry had offered to help them carry the painting upstairs. 'That's Chris's room.'

'What's the trouble?' Paul asked Mrs Mangel, who was looking quite stern.

'Far be it from me to eavesdrop on private conversations,'

she said rather haughtily. 'But they *were* shouting at each other. And in the interests of the other guests, I did think you should be informed.'

'Who was shouting?' Helen demanded.

'Mister and Mrs Wilton, of course.'

'Mister Wilton? She didn't say she had a husband.'

'Well, he's there now,' Mrs Mangel sniffed. 'And he's shouting at her. It seems he found her in . . . unseemly circumstances with the Mitchell boy. Oh, he was very angry—and rightly so, in my opinion. I shouldn't be surprised if there's some violence.'

'Come on, Paul.' Helen was running for the door. 'My painting's in there.'

They could hear the noise all the way along the corridor as they ran towards the door of room 203. Chris Wilton's voice rose shrilly from behind the door. 'How long has it been since you spent any time with me?' she was demanding. 'A woman *likes* a little masculine company at times.'

Then a man's voice was shouting back at her with a marked American accent. 'Do you call *this bozo* masculine company? And where exactly do *you* fit into this? You're sure as hell no painter.'

'Chris and I met in the bar this afternoon.' That was Henry's voice, a little shaky and very much on the defensive.

'You don't waste any time, do you?' Mister Wilton was apparently addressing Mrs Wilton again. 'What did you do? Call up and order him in advance?'

Frantic at the thought that her painting could be irreparably damaged in any ensuing mêlée, Helen rapped urgently at the door. 'Chris?' she called. 'Henry?'

But the row was still raging inside, and she hadn't been heard. Chris was almost screaming by now. 'I don't have to order *anyone*. *Some* people find me quite attractive as it is.'

'These Americans,' Mrs Mangel murmured as Helen began to pound on the door of room 203. 'So vulgar.'

'Henry, can you hear me?' Helen cried. 'Are you all right?'

This time Henry heard her. 'I'm okay, Mrs Daniels,' he called back as husband and wife continued to rage at each other. 'But they won't let me out.'

'Can you get the painting out?'

'I don't think so.' His voice came from just the other side of the door.

Helen turned to her grandson who was standing just behind her with a concerned expression. 'Paul, open the door,' she ordered. 'You have a key.'

'But, Gran, I can't just go barging in there,' he demurred. 'The guests are entitled to their privacy.'

'But the opening is in less than an hour,' Helen wailed. 'I *must* have that painting.'

'I'm sorry, Gran,' Paul said flatly. 'It's hotel policy.'

'But if they get . . . physical,'—Helen was absolutely desperate by now—'They might destroy it.'

'Then there would be no great harm done.' The satisfied gleam in Mrs Mangel's eyes abruptly vanished when Helen and Paul glared at her.

Helen turned back to her grandson who was being so ridiculously adamant about all this. 'Please, Paul . . .'

Paul relented just a fraction. 'If I hear anything being broken,' he said, 'I'll open up. But not before then.'

On the other side of the door, Henry was pleading with the warring couple who broke off hostilities just long enough to shout at him with one voice to keep out of it before taking up again where they had left off.

'Come on, Gran,' Paul said, taking Helen's arm. 'We'll go back to the office. I'll call them from there. Perhaps we can talk someone into opening the door.'

Reluctantly, Helen allowed herself to be led back along the passage, leaving Mrs Mangel to hover by the door of the room which was currently the scene of so much drama.

From the office, Helen tried to call the room again. When she still received no answer, Paul told her to keep trying. If she still couldn't get through, he would have to open the room. But he hoped it wouldn't need to come to that. Helen dialled the room number again. This time, to her relief, it was answered.

'Yes?' It was Chris's voice that came curtly on the line. In the background, Helen could hear the voice of Chris's husband who was presumably haranguing the unfortunate Henry.

'Chris, it's me, Helen. Just what is going on up there? The exhibition opens in half an hour, and I desperately need that portrait.'

In the background, the irate Mister Wilton shouted something about pretty boys. 'Shut up a minute,' Chris yelled before her voice came back on the line. 'The painting's fine, Helen,' she said tersely. 'The housekeeper just picked it up. Talk to you later.'

Breathing a huge sigh of relief, Helen replaced the receiver as the line went dead. 'It's okay,' she told Paul. 'She's given it to the housekeep . . .' Oh God, the housekeeper. Helen felt suddenly numb. 'She's given it to Mrs Mangel,' she moaned in total dismay.

There was no time to lose; she had to catch Mrs Mangel before she did something drastic with that painting. She made a dash to the door, leaving a startled Paul staring after her with his mouth open, and sprinted along the corridor to the main entrance. She darted past pillars and pot plants. People stared after her as she raced out through the entrance. She stopped briefly to look around for any sign of the absconding portrait-snatcher, then saw her hurrying across the bridge over the ornamental lake with the painting under her arm. Helen ran to head her off.

'Nell, give me that painting.'

'Not on your life.' Mrs Mangel clutched the painting possessively to her.

With the portrait between them, the two women faced each other on the bridge. It was a stand-off. Every time Helen advanced on her, Mrs Mangel backed away. Helen knew that Mrs Mangel was quite capable of throwing the portrait into the lake if she made a sudden rush for her. This was a matter for patience and gentle diplomacy.

'You may as well save your breath, Mrs Daniels,' Mrs Mangel said grimly. '*Nothing* will induce me to allow myself to become a figure of ridicule.'

'Nell, it's the last thing I want.'

'Pardon me if I find that difficult to believe.' Mrs Mangel's laugh bore not a trace of humour. 'I know you Robinsons.'

And the Robinsons knew Mrs Mangel—but this was not the time to engage in discussion of personalities. Helen was finding it extremely difficult to keep her patience with this silly, obstinate woman. 'Do you know who Mrs Wilton is?' she asked.

'I have already seen *what* she is,' Mrs Mangel rejoined in an icy tone.

'She's a respected art critic,' Helen informed her. 'She's here in Erinsborough to locate examples of representative Australian art for a major exhibition in New York.' Noting the faint glimmer of curiosity in Mrs Mangel's eyes, Helen saw an advantage and ruthlessly began to pursue it. 'And it just so happens that she's very impressed with that portrait. Oh, I know the style doesn't appeal to you,' she went on quickly when she saw that Mrs Mangel was about to say something. 'But there was a purpose to it. You see . . .' Now she began to lay it on a little thick, but not too thick, she hoped, not to set the other woman's imagination afire . . . 'I wanted to create the Australian spirit, the strength and determination of a true pioneer.' Mrs Mangel was no longer looking so grimly determined; her eyes had begun to take on a faraway expression. Helen went on relentlessly. 'The pride and resilience which has made our country great. I wanted the world to know about our self-sacrificing, courageous womanhood, of which . . .' and now came the clincher . . . 'you are such a shining example.'

There was now a definite light in the eyes of the shining example. 'I have had my trials,' she said with a touch of pride in her voice.

'And Chris *sees* all that in the portrait,' Helen said fervently. 'So . . . can we, in all conscience, let this opportunity pass us by?' Her voice took on a low and thrilling vibrancy. 'Can we let out nation down, Nell?'

And, of course, Mrs Mangel was unable to resist this appeal to her patriotism. Her eyes glistened; she gulped once, then again. Without a word, she allowed Helen to approach her across the bridge and gently relieve her of the painting.

The exhibition was well attended. Chris Wilton and her husband, with whom she had apparently made up in the meantime—or perhaps it was merely an armed truce—were there, as was Mrs Mangel, dressed to the nines and looking particularly indomitable. Helen recognised a couple of important art critics. People circulated and sipped wine; they nibbled savouries and passed comments on the paintings in muted voices; they fulsomely greeted friends and acquaintances, and smiled a lot; they clustered around the portrait of Mrs Mangel, the hardy woman pioneer, the centrepiece of the exhibition, which had been hung with barely a moment to spare. It seemed to be going especially well.

'Yes, isn't it?' Chris Wilton said when Helen made this observation to her. 'Quite a success.' She glanced across at Mrs Mangel who was hovering near her portrait and looking quite important. 'Your Mrs Mangel is quite insistent that her picture is going to New York. She was telling me about the insurance she will need to take out for such a valuable work of art.'

Helen looked at her sharply. 'Has she any reason to doubt that it will be going to New York?'

Chris's smile faded; she was suddenly serious, and while people drifted around them with glasses in their hand, Helen already sensed the rejection that was about to come. 'Look, Helen,' Chris said quietly, 'I'm afraid I won't be taking any of your pieces back with me.' Helen stared at her. Chris tried to soften the blow. 'Oh, they're charming, they really are. I like them very much. But there's something missing . . . There's nothing about it that's uniquely Helen Daniels.'

'Well, I suppose you're right.' Helen was trying very hard not to show her disappointment. 'I've been trying a number of different styles lately.'

'I know,' Chris said soberly. 'But if you were younger,

you would have . . . time to develop, to find that vitality and vibrancy the younger artists are able to achieve.'

Helen knew she was right, but that it didn't make it any easier. 'So . . . what you're saying is that you don't want to show what I paint.'

'I'm afraid that *is* what I'm saying,' Chris said as a burst of laughter from the other side of the room seemed particularly mocking to Helen just at that moment.

Before she could say anything more, Jim came up to them with a broad smile. 'Come on, Helen. It's time for you to make a little speech.'

It was the last thing Helen felt like doing right then, but she forced herself to smile. 'Oh, I'll be right there.'

As she was turning away, Chris stopped her. 'Don't feel too bad about it, Helen,' she said gently. 'Your work does give pleasure to a great many people. Just accept that and enjoy it.'

Helen glanced across at the portrait of Mrs Mangel. Suddenly, it was no longer the spirit of fierce indomitability in the face of hardship. She thought she was seeing it for the first time for what it actually was. A daub, she reflected bitterly. Yes, it was nothing more than a daub with too much purple in it.

Seven

It had taken much organisation and hard work to have the convention of travel agents staged at the hotel—and now, right on the eve of the convention, which could well put the hotel on the international map, and with its organiser due to arrive at any moment to check over the facilities, the staff had gone and called a strike. It was nothing more than sabotage, a bloody-minded act of destruction. Paul was furious.

It was that trouble-making chef, Dean Bartholomew, who was behind it. He was the one who had elected himself the spokesman; he was the one who had stirred them up to take militant action if Paul wasn't prepared to have Mrs Mangel reinstated in her job as the hotel housekeeper. But Paul had been adamant; he would not reconsider his decision to fire Mrs Mangel whose talkativeness had caused a great deal of mischief.

'Well, in that case, we don't care if you have a convention or not' the self-appointed spokesman said with some officiousness. 'As from now, the entire Lassiter's staff is officially on strike.'

Faced with this situation, the first thing Paul needed was time. He called his grandmother at home. 'We've got a strike on our hands,' he informed her. 'And the chauffeurs have gone out in sympathy. Now, Gran,' he went on quickly to forestall the questions Helen Daniels was already beginning to ask, 'the important thing now is that someone has to pick up Mister Elliott from the airport. Do you mind?'

'No . . . of course not.' At the other end of the line, Helen sounded a little wary.

'Great.' There was one problem out of the way at least. 'His plane gets in at five o'clock. And if you could buy me a little time . . .'

'The full guided tour,' Helen said. 'Leave it to me.'

'Thanks, Gran. Much appreciated.' With a relieved smile, Paul replaced the receiver.

'Paul, this is not going to work,' Gail Lewis said with a concerned frown.

'Well, it must.' Paul's smile faded as he looked across the office to Gail who didn't at that moment seem to possess the optimism one might have expected from a girl who had been hired as a publicity assistant. 'Do you realise how much extra business we should get from this Travel Agents' Association?'

'Why don't you tell Mister Elliott the truth?' Gail suggested. 'I'm sure he'll be sympathetic.'

'Oh, sure, sure,' Paul returned dubiously. 'And then he'll advise his members to stay somewhere more reliable.' He stared bleakly at his publicity assistant. 'Gail, I'm on trial here—can't you see that?'

'Yes, of course . . .'

There was a tap on the door, then Madge Mitchell marched briskly into the office. Paul looked up at her unexpectantly. 'Any luck?' he asked.

'No.' Madge shook her head. 'The entire staff seems to have gone.'

'Wonderful,' Paul groaned.

'There *is* a simple solution,' Gail pointed out to him.

'What's that?'

'Swallow your pride and give Mrs Mangel back her job.'

Paul slammed the flat of his hand on the desk in front of him. 'I will *not* give in to blackmail,' he exclaimed with some force. 'Look, I've got to cover this for twenty four hours . . . somehow.' He thought of something. 'Gail, would you go over to Reception and put out the "No Vacancy" sign. The last thing I need right now are additional guests.'

'Sure.' Gail hurried out of the room.

Madge was still standing just inside the door. 'Paul, the supplies for tonight's banquet have been delivered to the service area,' she said. 'I had better put them in the kitchen.'

Tonight's banquet—hah! A crowd of travel agents sampling the superbly cooked bill-of-fare, sipping the finest wines . . . Paul was on his feet, taking off his jacket. 'That's a man's job. Unless, of course, you think that's sexist.'

'It never crossed my mind.' Madge's face was quite devoid of expression.

'And could you round up as many of the staff as you can? I want to have a meeting.'

'Perhaps you could call the agencies for temporary staff,' Madge suggested. 'I know it's short notice, but . . .'

'If I do that,' Paul interrupted her, 'then that maniac chef of mine will organise a picket line outside the hotel. No, thanks.'

What to do? What to do? They would need eight people at least, to look after the banquet alone. 'How would you feel about preparing a banquet for a group of one hundred and fifty travel agents hot off the plane from Fiji?' Gail asked Madge.

'Are we that desperate?'

'Oh . . . it's just the tip of the iceberg.'

'What about professional caterers?'

'There isn't the time.'

'What we need,' Paul said glumly, 'is a miracle.'

'A miracle . . .' Madge was suddenly looking extremely thoughtful. She snapped her fingers. 'A Ramsay Street miracle, she exclaimed.

The alarm bells were already beginning to sound. 'Now, Madge, hold on there . . .'

But Madge was already becoming enthused with her idea. 'It will work, Paul,' she assured him brightly. 'Daphne and I can handle the cooking. Charlene and Henry will help. And Scott has had experience in the coffee shop . . .'

'But this is a gourmet banquet,' Paul protested wildly. 'Not hamburgers and chips . . .'

97

'Hamburgers and . . .' Madge frowned at him in reproach. 'Don't be so negative. And it's only for one night.'

One for one night . . . It hadn't taken the *Titanic* anywhere near that long to sink to the bottom of the ocean. 'Have you got any alternative suggestions, Paul?' Gail queried.

Paul had to admit he hadn't. But one thing he did know was that when Ramsay Street decided to pull together in a moment of crisis, they normally pulled in five different directions. He was suddenly filled with a sense of gloomy foreboding.

After consigning Jane Harris to the main switchboard to contact everyone, Madge set out to organise things in the kitchen. 'One hundred and fifty!' Daphne exclaimed when Madge told her how many people were expected for dinner.

'We'll cope,' Madge said with more hope than confidence. 'I mean, it's a buffet. There's a menu all laid out.'

'I'd better have a look.'

While Daphne was having a look, her husband Des was offering his services to Paul. 'You name it, I'll do it. Head-waiter perhaps . . . ?'

A list had already been drawn up. 'What have we got down for Des?' Paul asked Gail.

Gail consulted the list. 'Kitchen hand. Dishwasher.'

Des's mouth fell open. 'Dishwasher?'

'I guess it's not impossible,' Daphne was saying to Madge. 'Your seafood would win prizes.'

Madge returned the compliment. 'Not to mention your pavlova.'

There wasn't much time; they had about forty five minutes before Helen arrived with Elliott from the airport. Becoming increasingly frazzled, and with his fingers crossed, Paul directed the frantic preparations in the restaurant. People were scurrying everywhere, bumping into each other and tripping over things. Scott Robinson had already changed into a waiter's uniform, but Henry Mitchell and Mike Young were having some trouble finding starched jackets to fit them. Charlene was looking particularly fetching in a skimpy black dress with white frills. Madge and Daphne were having a slight difference of opinion.

'I'm telling you—you put the rack of lamb on a low heat and let it broil. Especially with a sauce like that.'

'Oh come off it, Madge. You have to sear the meat first, before you lower the heat.'

Charlene was complaining about her abbreviated costume; the air conditioning was giving her goose-bumps. 'You're supposed to look foxy for all those businessmen,' Scott said with a smirk at her cleavage.

'One smart remark,' Charlene retorted, 'and they can *wear* their soup.'

There was such a commotion in the room; everyone was talking at once. Paul yelled for silence. 'We've got to get ourselves organised,' he said when the hubbub had died down enough for him to make himself heard. 'This isn't going to work unless you all do as you're told, and stop messing around.'

'Just remember we're doing you a favour, mate,' Scott called across the room to him.

'And just remember that you're being paid for it,' Paul shot back.

Madge was offended. 'Oh, now come on, Paul. I'm sure none of us is doing it for the money.'

'I know, I know . . . I'm sorry.' Paul sighed; it was all such a tremendous strain on him, trying to keep an eye on everything at once. He tried to make them understand how important it was that the banquet was a success. 'If these guys like Lassiter's, then we will be upgraded and included in their package deals. We're talking international tourism here. The stakes are very high. Can you all understand that?'

There were murmurs and some sheepish nods. 'We won't let you down, Paul,' Daphne promised.

'Fine. Thanks.'

At that point, Gail rushed in with some disturbing news for Paul. There were problems, she told him. 'Helen has just called. They'll be here in about ten minutes. Apparently, Mister Elliott didn't want to do any sightseeing and insisted on coming straight here. Another thing—he knows all about Dean Bartholomew's reputation as a chef and expects to meet him.

'You're kidding.' Paul suddenly felt queasy. This was a complication he just did not need.

'Someone will have to pretend to be Dean,' Gail said. 'What else can we do?'

Paul's eyes lit on Des who had just wandered in to ask how many potatoes he needed to peel. 'Des, you'll have to be the chef.'

Des brightened from the gloom that had descended on him with the information that he would need to peel enough potatoes for one hundred and fifty people. 'Whatever you want,' he said, then a thought struck him. 'Do I have to cook?'

'No,' Paul assured him. 'All you have to do is talk about it a bit when you meet Bernard Elliott. Right?'

'Right.'

Everybody had moved to their stations, but the scene was only marginally less chaotic than before. While Madge supervised the bubbling pots on the stove, Mike and Scott and Henry were hauling an assortment of vegetables from the cold room, Charlene was experiencing some difficulty in folding the linen serviettes, and Daphne stirred the sauce and briefed Des, who by now was dressed in a chef's uniform, on the rudiments of the craft.

'Now repeat after me. French cuisine needed new direction, but Nouvelle Cuisine went too far.'

'French cuisine needed . . . What is it supposed to mean?'

'You don't have to know what it means. It sounds very stylish. Mister Elliott wants to be impressed. What's a roux?'

'A marsupial?'

'It's the base for a sauce.'

'Oh.'

Madge had her own pennyworth to add to the instruction of Des in the culinary arts. 'Now listen, Des,' she said impressively, 'when this man gets here, there will be a pot of sauce simmering on the stove. While you're talking to him, give it a stir, then tell either Daphne or myself that it needs more . . . texture.'

'Texture.' Des nodded slowly. 'Yeah, right . . .'

'Texture.'

Charlene had given up struggling with the serviettes. 'Mum, I can't do these properly.'

'Forget it then. We'll use napkin rings instead.' Madge checked the menu. 'Daphne, what on earth is Chicken Lassiter?'

'Beats me,' Daphne shrugged. 'Probably one of Dean's secret recipes. We'll fake it with my lemon sauce.'

Madge called across to Scott. 'Fifteen lemons, please.'

'Coming right up. Scott tossed a lemon to Henry who tossed it to Mike who tossed it to Madge. He picked up another lemon.

Paul was quite philosophical about it when he came into the room with Gail and saw the lemons flying through the air; he was almost beyond pain by now. 'Oh perfect,' he said drily. 'Now they're working on the floor show.'

'It's all happening—that's what matters.' Gail clapped her hands together. 'Okay, Charlene . . . guys . . . take up your places. They'll be here in a minute.'

Paul moved across to Daphne. 'Is everything all right?'

Daphne gave him a fleeting smile as she stirred the sauce. 'It'll be all right on the night.'

'Paul,' Gail called to him. 'Let them get on with it.'

'I could be out of my mind,' Paul groaned.

It had been arranged that the hotel's regular guests be given meal vouchers and sent across to the Royal Hotel for their dinner. At the reception desk, Jane was just handing out the last of these when Eileen Clarke came in through the main entrance. She was startled to see Jane behind the desk. 'What are you doing there?' she demanded.

If things were bad enough already, they were hardly likely to be improved by the arrival of Mrs Clarke. 'Filling in . . .'

Mrs Clarke glanced sharply around her. 'Has the whole place gone mad? I go to the coffee shop and find it locked.

101

I go to Paul's office, and he's gone. The whole complex looks like a morgue . . .' She descended on Paul and Gail who had just emerged from the passage leading to the restaurant. 'What *is* going on here?'

Eileen Clarke was the last person Paul wanted to see at this time of intense crisis. 'Eileen, could you go somewhere . . . anywhere . . .' he gestured in exasperation . . . 'I don't care. We haven't got time.'

'But why is the coffee shop locked? Where's Daphne?'

'She's in the hotel kitchen.'

'What?'

Henry Mitchell who had been posted to watch out for the arrival of Helen and the man from the Travel Association, darted in through the door. 'They're here.'

Eileen looked at him. 'Who?'

'Not now, Eileen,' Paul said as he and Gail hurried outside to greet their important guest.

Eileen wheeled on Jane who was looking rather nervous. 'Jane, I demand an explanation,' she said in a voice that brooked no opposition.

Bernard Elliott of the Travel Association was a somewhat fussy man of indeterminate appearance. 'Well, that remains to be seen, doesn't it?' he said a little stuffily when Gail offered the hope that he would enjoy his stay at the hotel.

'Perhaps you would like to make a brief inspection of our facilities,' Paul suggested hopefully.

Elliott's smile was faintly patronising. 'I can assure you my inspection of this place will be exhaustive,' he said. 'We like to be absolutely certain before we place our seal of approval on an establishment.'

'Of course.' Paul tried to appear nonchalant, as if this presented no problem at all.

Henry had already taken Elliott's bags up to the Arcadia Suite which had been set aside for him. Paul and Gail were shepherding their honoured guest towards the main doors when they suddenly slid open and there, facing them with a broad, welcoming smile, was Eileen Clarke. She swept grandly towards them. 'Dear Mister Elliott,' she greeted him in a voice that positively dripped with sincerity. 'May

I say what an honour it is to have you and your Association as our guests.'

Paul and Gail had suddenly gone rigid. What now? What further catastrophe was about to be heaped on them? Inwardly, Paul was cringing. Why him? Why was all this happening to him?

'Why . . . thank you.' Elliott was looking slightly confused. Paul stepped forward.

'Oh . . . this is Mrs Clarke . . .'

'That's right,' Eileen interrupted smoothly. 'I'm the housekeeper here at Lassiter's.' Her smile was voraciously friendly. 'I think we can show you a few surprises.'

Paul stared after them dismally as, taking Elliott's arm, Eileen led him into the hotel. Surprises, she had said. They were there, all right—an abundance of them. 'Why me, Gail?' he asked brokenly. 'Why does it have to be me?'

In the foyer, when Bernard Elliott commented on the fact that the hotel seemed to be light on staff, Gail was quick to provide an explanation. 'We prefer to keep the service unobtrusive . . . but complete. We think the guests can feel overwhelmed if the staff is overly attentive.'

'But our clients like to be spoilt,' Elliott said pointedly. 'At least I hope that's what you meant.'

'Naturally,' Gail said. 'Which is why we spared no pains to secure a chef of Dean Bartholomew's outstanding reputation.' Her smile radiated confidence. 'Tonight's menu will be very special.'

'Good.' Elliott's head inclined in a small, satisfied nod. 'Now I would like to see the restaurant, if you wouldn't mind.'

As Gail led him off in the direction of the restaurant, Eileen was about to follow them when Paul abruptly hauled her back. 'Oh no you don't,' he growled. 'I want an explanation, and I want it now.'

'Well . . .' Eileen shook herself free of Paul's restraining hand. 'When I heard that the whole street was pitching in, I decided to give you a hand . . . and I thought the best way to do that was stand in as the housekeeper.'

'All right, all right . . .' It was too late to worry about

that now; the damage had already been done. 'All right, but just try not to talk to Mister Elliott. He knows this business inside out, so just leave it to us to handle him.'

'Paul.' Eileen gave him an affronted look. 'Would I interfere?'

With a sigh, Paul hurried after Gail and Elliott who were just entering the restaurant where, the call for action stations having been given, everyone was trying to look reasonably professional.

Elliott wasn't impressed by the buffet arrangement. 'It strikes me as being a little inelegant,' he observed stiffly to Paul.

'Not at all,' Paul hastily assured him. 'Every dish will be of gourmet quality—naturally. And it gives your group a chance to sample a variety of Mister Bartholomew's cuisine without imposing a set menu, or . . . or amounts of food on tired guests who may have already eaten on the plane.'

'Yes, of course.' Now Elliott was impressed. 'Excellent. I like that degree of care.' He eyed Charlene, Scott and Mike who were standing rather awkwardly to attention. 'You staff doesn't look terribly experienced, however.'

Paul gulped, and thought quickly. 'Well . . . you see . . . my policy is that young people add to the attraction of a meal well presented. Under the correct training and supervision, of course.'

Elliott was still looking doubtfully at the three teenagers. 'Risky, I would say,' he murmured. 'Anyway, we'll find out tonight, won't we?' Paul gulped again. We would, he thought miserably. 'Now I would like to confer with the chef,' Elliott said.

'Yes, of course,' Paul said. 'I'll show you around on the way to the kitchen.'

'Gourmet food is something of a hobby of mine,' Elliott remarked as Paul began to lead him away. 'I regard people like Bartholomew as artists—absolute artists.'

'Only the best will do,' Paul agreed.

In the kitchen, Des was chopping up onions and repeating to himself, 'Classical French cuisine, classical French cuisine . . .'

'Classic, not classical,' Daphne said as she brought another tray of pavlovas from the oven. 'Madge, how's the lamb?'

'You were right,' Madge said glumly.

Daphne shrugged. 'Everyone gets lucky.'

Charlene hurried in from the restaurant. 'Paul's giving Elliott the grand tour,' she announced a little breathlessly. 'You've got about two minutes.'

Scott rushed in behind her. 'Everything's set up out there.' He pulled up in front of Daphne. 'Er . . . Daph, what else can I do?'

'Take over the onions,' Daphne told him. 'Des, wipe your eyes.'

'Classic French cuisine, classic French cuisine . . .'

'Des, you can do it,' Madge said. 'The worst is over.'

Eileen Clarke bustled into the kitchen. 'Don't panic. Don't panic. I'm here.'

Madge was the first to recover from the general astonishment at Eileen's appearance. She pointed to the door. 'Eileen . . . *out*.'

Eileen stood her ground. 'Don't you get high-handed with me,' she said sharply. 'It just so happens that I am standing in as housekeeper here.' She smiled proudly at her son. 'Desmond, you look wonderful as a chef.'

Daphne tried the diplomatic approach without any real hope of it being successful. 'Eileen, please . . . We've got it all arranged. You would be much more helpful in the restaurant.'

Eileen was examining the trays of pavlovas. 'These should be refrigerated for a start,' she stated firmly.

'I haven't finished decorating them yet,' Daphne muttered through clenched teeth.

'Oh, we mustn't leave them out in the heat.' Picking up one of the pavlovas, Eileen handed it to a startled Charlene. 'Put them in the fridge,' she ordered.

'Charlene, put it back,' Daphne commanded.

'Don't be stubborn, Daphne.' Eileen turned back to Charlene who by now was quite confused. 'Now, come on, do as you're told. Put them in the fridge.'

Holding onto the pavlova, the hapless Charlene was turning one way then the other as the orders were barked at her. She was just turning back from Eileen to Daphne when Mike rushed in and collided with the pavlova. He looked down in dismay at his smeared jacket. 'You idiot,' he cried.

'It was an accident.'

'You did it on purpose.'

'I did not.'

'Quiet,' Daphne yelled as the argument became more heated. 'Eileen, take Mike and clean him up. And the rest of you . . . stay calm.'

In the meantime, Paul and Gail were continuing to stall Bernard Elliott, who was becoming increasingly impatient. They showed him all around the hotel, and Paul talked enthusiastically of the renovations he intended to make. They were fast running out of diversionary tactics. 'Well now, perhaps a stroll through the office area,' Paul suggested hopefully.

'For the third time,' Elliott said shortly, 'I want to see the kitchen. And I want to see Dean Bartholomew.'

'Perhaps after dinner this evening . . .'

'Dean is very temperamental,' Gail quickly supplied. 'As you said, he's an artist. He won't have people in his kitchen.'

Elliott chuckled. 'Dean may complain, but I don't think he'll throw me out,' he said. 'We go back too far together.'

Now what was he saying? He couldn't be saying . . . 'You . . . you . . . you go back?' Paul queried with a tremor in his voice. 'You know Dean personally then?' He was silently praying that Elliott would say it wasn't so.

Elliott said it was so. 'I told you about my interest in food,' he explained. 'It was through that that I met Dean . . . oh, about five years ago. We've been close friends ever since. Now,' he went on briskly as Paul and Gail exchanged a slow, frozen glance, 'the kitchen.'

Dead ducks— that was what they were. 'Stall him,' Paul hissed to Gail as Elliott began to wander away from them. 'For God's sake, stall him.'

Elliott turned back to them. 'What's that?'

'I've . . . ah . . . just realised that I have to go to the office after all,' Paul said hurriedly.

'I see.'

Paul was thinking fast. 'A telex confirmation of a booking. I want to make sure it's there.'

Elliott nodded understandingly. 'Of course.'

Paul edged away from him. 'I'll only be a few minutes.' He gestured towards Gail. 'And I can assure you I'm leaving you in very capable hands.'

Gail took it from there. 'Yes, and perhaps on the way to the kitchen I could point out a couple of landscaping features which I'm sure you'll find interesting.'

Paul hoped so; he fervently hoped so as he hurried off to see what could be retrieved from the shambles.

In the restaurant, the food was being arranged on the buffet table. Admiring the array, Des was the only one not engaged in frantic activity. 'Oh, Des,' Paul called urgently as he came into the room. 'Des . . .'

Des corrected him. 'It's Dean—remember?'

'Not any more, pal. You're Des.'

'How come?'

'Because the situation has changed, that's how come.'

'Well, who's Dean then?'

'Dean is.'

Daphne scuttled in from the kitchen with two of her pavlovas. 'Gail has just brought Mister Elliott into the kitchen through the back way,' she cried to Des. 'So for heaven's sake, get out there and act like a chef.'

Paul gaped at her in horror. 'How do I look?' Des asked. 'Fine, fine,' Paul mumbled. 'No, no . . . that's all right.'

Hearing footsteps behind them, they swung quickly as Gail and Bernard Elliott entered from the kitchen. Elliott looked around the room expectantly. 'Is Dean not here?'

'Yeah,' Des said, then remembered he was no longer Dean. 'Ah . . . no.'

'Desmond is Dean's assistant, actually,' Paul said quickly, then introduced Desmond to Bernard Elliott. 'Mister Elliott is an old friend of Dean's,' he explained in a voice loud enough for Madge and Daphne to hear as they

107

were on their way back to the kitchen. With a startled glance at each other, they stopped and listened.

'That's nice,' Desmond said uncertainly.

'It's a shame that Dean had to go out, actually.' Pointedly, Paul looked around at the others. 'Isn't it?'

Madge and Daphne spoke at once. 'To the bar,' Madge said.

'To the dining room,' Daphne said.

'To the bar on the way to the dining room,' Madge amended.

Daphne nodded. 'That's right.'

Bernard Elliott didn't seem to notice their agitation. 'Well, I expect to catch up with him sooner or later,' he said. He smiled at Des. 'He's a superb chef. I'm really looking forward to sampling his food again.'

'Really?' Des asked weakly.

'Yes, and there's one dish in particular . . .' Elliott considered for a moment. 'Chicken fillets with a natural asparagus sauce. For the life of me, I can't remember what he calls it.

'Chicken Asparagus?' Des suggested.

Paul gave him a sharp nudge in the ribs. 'Er . . . Elegant Supreme,' he hazarded.

'That's the one.' Elliott beamed at him. 'A marvellous marriage of flavours.' He turned back to Des. 'I suppose you also have your specialities.'

Des looked cornered. 'I imagined so,' he murmured.

Daphne stepped forward to be helpful. 'Desmond is being very modest,' she said. 'He does a very wonderful chicken dish himself. It's a . . . a type of Lemon Chicken.'

'Lemon Chicken?' Elliott didn't seem to be particularly impressed.

Daphne went on undaunted. 'Chicken Lassiter he calls it. You really have to taste it to know how wonderful it is.'

'Well, I hope I soon have the privilege.' Looking around the room, Elliott appeared satisfied with what he saw. 'I must say that I'm most impressed with the staff and the kitchen,' he remarked to Paul. He chuckled. 'It seems that

Dean is still running a tight ship. That's very good, that's excellent. He was always a one for efficiency.'

'Yes, he is.' Paul managed a faint smile.

'Which is as it should be,' Elliott continued. 'I mean, after all, it does reflect on the entire hotel, doesn't it?'

Paul's smile was in danger of becoming a permanent fixture. 'Yes,' he said, 'very much so.'

Gail had taken Elliott to the bar. More platters of food were brought from the kitchen to be arranged on the buffet. Des argued with Henry over the salad vegetables and the size of the pieces into which they should be chopped. 'If you cut them any smaller,' Des said knowingly, 'they'll need tweezers to eat them.'

'This is the way you're supposed to do it.'

'Yeah'

'Yeah'

Picking up a meat cleaver, Des began to chop some carrots into large chunks, while Henry pointedly decimated some parsnips into very small chunks. Daphne was staring in dismay at her sauce which had curdled. She kicked the stove in frustration just as Dean Bartholomew made an enraged entrance into the kitchen.

'This is my kitchen,' he yelled to the startled gathering, 'and I want you out of here.'

Henry was holding his knife, and Des his meat cleaver. 'We're not going anywhere, mate,' Henry said evenly.

'Scabs!' Dean Bartholomew's face was very red. He pointed an accusing finger. 'You're nothing but scabs—all of you.'

'We are not,' Charlene cried. 'You called an illegal strike.'

Madge smiled approvingly at her daughter who knew the rights and wrongs of things. 'You tell him, love.'

'Very well.' Dean Bartholomew glared at them all menacingly through narrowed eyes. 'I'll see what Mister Bernard Elliott has to say about this.'

Without really being aware that he was doing it, except perhaps to emphasise a point, Des brandished the meat cleaver as he advanced on the outraged chef. 'Actually, we would rather you didn't,' he said.

Dean Bartholomew was backing away from him. 'We've done a lot of hard work here,' Daphne supplied, 'and I think it's pretty mean of you to want to ruin it.'

'So we would like you to reconsider.' Henry still had the knife in his hand.

Behind Bartholomew was the walk-in pantry. Seeing a chance, Charlene opened the door. The others had formed a half-circle around the chef who was now looking a little apprehensive. 'Look here . . .'

'But as you don't want to talk about it, I guess we'll have to use other means.' Before Bartholomew realised what was happening, Henry gave him a hearty push with the flat of the hand that wasn't holding the knife. Bartholomew staggered backwards into the pantry. Henry quickly slammed the door and bolted it.

'Henry,' Madge cried out in a shocked voice when she saw what her son had done. 'What have you done? You're on parole.'

'It was self-defence, Mum,' Charlene remarked.

'But it's kidnapping. Or something.'

Henry's shrug was quite offhand. 'Kidnapping, false imprisonment, assault—take your pick.'

Des smiled at him weakly. 'In for a penny, in for a pound—eh, Henry?'

'Right,' Henry agreed with a decisive nod. 'Only we have five witnesses to say it never happened, including a bank manager and woman with child.'

'That's me,' Daphne said with a pleasant smile.

But Madge was still having her doubts. 'I still think we should let him out.'

Dean was banging loudly on the pantry door and demanding to be released. 'A rat in a trap,' Charlene said proudly.

Madge glanced at the pantry door which was shaking a little under Dean Bartholomew's fierce assault on it. 'And we will let him out,' she said. 'Immediately after dinner.'

Charlene grinned at her. 'That's my Mum.'

Dean was swearing savage revenge. 'I'm with you, Madge,' Daphne said. 'So is Des.' Des wasn't looking so sure about that. 'Anyway, it was Dean's fault. He was the one who called the stupid strike in the first place.'

'Of course he did.' Charlene raised her voice so Dean could hear her. 'Hey, you'd better make yourself at home in there. You've got a long wait.'

With Dean Bartholomew safely locked away in the pantry, it was back to work; there were still things to be done before the arrival of the party of travel agents who might or might not be hungry. It had been agreed not to mention anything about Dean to Paul when he came to check the progress of the preparations. 'Well, well,' he said, looking at the buffet table with approval. 'I think you've saved my neck. I didn't realise you were all so talented.'

'Teamwork,' Charlene told him.

Madge gestured towards the warming tray. 'Paul, I don't know if this thing will keep the food hot enough,' she said with a worried frown. 'I do wish those travel agents would get a move on.'

'So do I,' Paul said, glancing at his watch. 'I don't know what the hold up is.'

Bernard Elliott joined them. 'Ah, most impressive,' he said, casting an appreciative eye over the buffet. 'Most impressive indeed. I must congratulate Dean.' He began to move towards the kitchen.

They had to stop him entering the kitchen where Dean Bartholomew was still presumably trying to batter down the pantry door. 'Mister Elliott,' Daphne said quickly, 'do you think the guests will be arriving soon?'

'I certainly hope so.' The move to distract him had been successful for the moment at least. 'Perhaps I should contact the airline,' Elliott suggested to Paul. 'There's obviously been some delay. I can only hope it's short-lived.'

'Yes.' Taking Elliott's arm, Paul turned him in the direction of the reception area. 'Either way, I think we should find out now.'

'Yes, quite,' Elliott said. 'Do give my apologies to Dean, won't you? He'll think I'm deliberately avoiding him.'

'I'm sure he'll understand.'

When Elliott had gone, there was a general sigh of relief. 'Whew, that was close,' Henry remarked.

'Yeah.' Charlene smiled feebly. 'I'll say.'

'Well, so far so good,' Paul observed briskly. 'Let's just hope that Dean doesn't make a sudden reappearance now.'

'Oh, he won't,' Charlene promised him.

Paul looked at her. 'You sound pretty definite about that.'

Charlene shrugged as the others glared at her. 'Woman's intuition,' she said brightly.

Within five minutes, Bernard Elliott was back, looking rather glum. 'Any news?' Paul asked him.

Elliott nodded. 'Bad.' Everyone stared at him; the collective breath was held. 'The plane from Fiji ran into trouble,' he explained. 'It had to turn back. They won't be arriving until tomorrow, unfortunately.'

Daphne gave a sharp cry of dismay. 'What?'

'And I apologise for the inconvenience,' Elliott said, then shrugged. 'But it just can't be helped.'

After he had left them again, it was a long time before anyone spoke. They were in a mild state of shock. After all the trouble they had taken, the preparations they had made, the nervous strain of it all . . . Henry was the first to break the silence. 'What a waste of time,' he said in disgust.

Daphne nodded. 'And food.'

'And money,' Paul observed sourly.

Paul snuffed out one of the candles that gave the tastefully laid out buffet table added allure. 'That's the last time *I* do any cooking,' he muttered.

Paul gestured forlornly towards the food. 'I wish there was something I could do about this,' he said, 'but there isn't. And I don't like the idea of all this food being thrown out, either.'

'Does it have to be thrown out?' Madge asked.

'There's a limit to what we can all eat,' Daphne remarked. She grimaced. 'Anyway, I can hardly bear to look at it now.'

'I wasn't thinking of us,' Madge said. 'Why can't we

throw a party for some of the local senior citizens? It wouldn't cost the hotel more than it has already.'

'That sounds like a good idea,' Paul said.

They discussed the matter in some detail. For the moment, anyway, they had quite forgotten that Dean Bartholomew was still locked in the kitchen pantry.

Eight

'I've got a job,' Charlene announced.

Scott was pleased for her; she had been trying so hard to find a job. 'As an apprentice motor mechanic?' It was what she had set her heart on becoming.

'Yeah . . .' Charlene nodded. She didn't seem to be particularly excited by the fact that she had found a job at last.

'Hey, that's great,' Scott exclaimed.

'Wait until you hear the rest,' Charlene said glumly. 'It's up in Brisbane. Uncle Max arranged it for me. I'll have to go up there to live.'

Scott stared at her in disbelief. Brisbane? That was hundreds of miles away. This wasn't so great after all. 'You're not taking it, are you? I mean, you just can't go off like that.'

'I can't get a job here,' Charlene said unhappily as she stirred the breakfast cereal she had hardly touched. 'And it *is* an apprenticeship. It's what I want to do. I just can't let it slip through my fingers.'

Scott was deeply hurt, but he tried not to show it. 'When are you leaving?'

'Mum has booked me on a bus for late this afternoon.'

'*Today?*' This was even worse.

Charlene nodded again. 'The guy who offered me the job has been looking for an apprentice,' she told him. 'He wants someone to start immediately. So . . . if I don't get there quickly, he'll give the job to someone else.'

'It's for three years, isn't it?' Scott couldn't keep the bitterness out of his voice. 'An apprenticeship?'

114

'But I won't have to be away that long,' Charlene assured him.

'After a year, I will probably have enough experience to get a job down here.'

'Probably?' It didn't sound very definite.

Charlene gave an awkward shrug. 'You can't be sure about things like that.'

'It seems to me you can't be sure about anything,' Scott said testily. 'I thought our relationship was important.'

'Don't be stupid,' Charlene snapped back at him. 'Of course it's important.' Her expression softened; she put down the spoon with which she had been toying. 'We'll be in touch all the time. You can come up during the holidays. It's only for a year or so.'

A year was a very long time. 'Lots of things can change in a year,' Scott said miserably. 'You might meet some other guy up there . . .'

'*You're* my boyfriend,' Charlene interrupted him. 'That won't change.'

Scott could hear Charlene's mother moving around in another part of the house; she had made herself scarce when Scott had arrived in response to Charlene's telephone call. 'I thought at least you could have talked to me before you made a decision,' Scott reproached Charlene. 'But now, you've got everything tied up. You're doing it. You're leaving this afternoon.' Abruptly pushing the chair back, he jumped to his feet and headed for the door. 'It's terrific,' he cried brokenly. 'Maybe I'll see you before you go.'

'Will you try and see it my way?' Charlene called after him. 'I don't *want* to leave you, but . . .'

Scott didn't hear the rest; he slammed the door behind him.

'That's a bit rough, mate,' Mike Young sympathised when Scott told him of Charlene's decision.

'I didn't think she would want to leave me.'

'Well, I don't really think she does,' Mike pointed out to him. 'But you can't really blame her, can you? She was becoming so depressed lately about not getting a job. She could hardly knock one back when it falls into her lap.'

Scott was giving Mike a lift to the university. He pulled up at a red light. 'Well, if it was me,' he muttered, '*I* wouldn't leave *her* like that—no matter what.'

'Look, mate,' Mike said in that faintly patronising tone he had adopted since he had begun attending the university, and which Scott felt all the more keenly now that he had decided to spend another year at school. 'Once you get out in the world you realise you have to take every chance you can.'

Scott gave him a scornful glance. 'A couple of weeks at uni and you're already talking about being out in the world.'

'It does change your attitude towards things a little.' There was a defensive edge to Mike's voice.

The lights changed; Scott eased the car forward. 'Thanks a lot, Mike,' he said, ruefully. 'I'm only stuck in school for another year. Charlene probably doesn't want to go out with a schoolkid any more . . .'

'I'm sorry, mate.' Mike touched him lightly on the arm. 'But it seems to me that if you love her, you have to let her go. You just can't stand in her way.'

Scott knew he was right, but it didn't make him feel any better about it. 'No, I guess not,' he murmured unhappily.

He decided not to go to school that day. Charlene would be leaving for Brisbane in a few hours and he needed to see her again. He found her ironing clothes in the kitchen. 'Why aren't you at school?' she demanded.

'I wouldn't be able to concentrate.'

Standing the iron up on the board, she crossed to him and gazed sombrely into his eyes. 'Scott, you know I don't want to leave you.'

Scot knew that. 'Yeah . . .'

'I promise I won't even look at another guy.'

He took her in his arms and held her tightly. 'I'll wait for you,' he said a little huskily. 'And I guess a year isn't such a long time. Anyway . . .' he smiled at her sadly . . . 'we can spend the rest of the day together, can't we?'

'Oh, I can't.' Charlene's expression clouded. 'Mum has taken time off work so we can go shopping.'

'Oh . . .' Scott was deeply disappointed.

Wearing a full-length slip and carrying a blouse, Madge Mitchell hurried into the room. 'Charlene, do you think you can run the iron over . . .' She broke off in surprise when she saw Scott who had abruptly broken the embrace with Charlene at her unexpected arrival. 'Oh . . . Scott . . . excuse me.' Quickly handing the blouse to Charlene, Madge was beating a hasty and embarrassed exit when she stopped briefly in the doorway. 'And don't you go upsetting Charlene,' she said sternly. 'The plans are made, and they can't be changed now.'

When she had gone, Scott took Charlene in his arms again. 'I'm sorry,' Charlene whispered. 'I really am sorry . . .'

Jim Robinson wasn't at all pleased that Scott had taken the day off from school. 'I know you're repeating the year,' he said tersely when Scott mooched into the house a short time later, 'but you can't afford to mess around . . .'

Scott almost yelled at his father. 'Listen, Dad, will you stop hassling me.'

'Hang on, hang on.' Jim held up a hand. 'What's up?'

Scott didn't really expect his father to understand, but he told him, anyway. 'It won't seem important to you,' he muttered, 'but Charlene is leaving. To Brisbane. For a year or longer.'

'Oh.' Jim was immediately sympathetic. 'That's a shame. You've been getting along so well lately.'

'Yeah, well . . .' Scott shook his head unhappily. 'She was offered an apprenticeship up there.'

Jim smiled. 'Good for her.'

'Yeah . . .'

'Oh come on, Scott.' Jim placed a hand on his son's shoulder. 'You can still keep in touch. It's not the end of the world, you know.'

'Maybe not. But we still won't see each other for a long time.'

'If there's anything I can do . . .'

'Thanks, Dad.'

'Do you want a cup of coffee, and we can talk about it?'

'I don't think I'd be really good company at the moment,' Scott murmured. 'I would prefer to be by myself.'

'Sure.'

In his room, Scott picked up the photograph of Charlene that stood on the bedside table, and gazed at it for a long time. Charlene . . . She was going away, and he wouldn't see her again for at least a year. Charlene, in her overalls and with a grease smudge on her face, always tinkering about with car engines; Charlene who said she loved him and had talked about getting married one day; Charlene who packed a mighty punch . . . Scott's eyes filled with tears.

He had fallen asleep on his bed. When he woke up, it was quite late. Bleary-eyed, he wandered out into the living room where his father was making notes on a series of plans laid out on the desk in front of him. 'I can't believe I slept so long . . .' He remembered something. 'Oh blast, there's not much time left to say goodbye to Charlene.'

'She was here,' Jim quietly informed him.

'What?' Scott was immediately alert. 'Why didn't you wake me?'

'She asked me not to. She felt it was best that way, that saying goodbye would be too upsetting for both of you. She said she would call you from Brisbane.'

'But I can't . . .' It wasn't right; he couldn't let her go just like that, without saying goodbye. 'I've *got* to see her.'

'They've already left for the bus terminal. In a taxi.'

Scott hurried to the door. 'Yeah, well . . .'

'Don't go driving like a maniac,' Jim called after him.

'Dad, I've got to see her,' Scott yelled as he sprinted along the hall to the front door.

He drove as fast as he could. He was tense; there was so little time to spare. He groaned in despair at every red light, or when the traffic moved too slowly. It seemed to him that he was hardly making any progress at all, just inching along in the traffic. Then finally, after what seemed hours but was in fact little more than twenty minutes, he was turning into the bus terminal with a faint protesting squeal from the tyres as he rounded the corner, and there . . . there . . .

118

He slammed his foot down on the brake pedal and stared in dismay at the bus which was just pulling out of the terminal. He was too late; Charlene was already on her way to Brisbane—and he hadn't had a chance to say goodbye to her. A lump began to form in his throat.

Then, as he was staring after the receding bus, now blurring a little through the stinging tears in his eyes, he noticed a lone figure standing on the platform. It was a girl, and she was staring across at him. There was a suitcase next to her. It was Charlene. With a whoop of joy, Scott wrenched open the door and leapt out of the car to rush across to Charlene, who hadn't been able to bear the thought of leaving him after all.

Nine

When Mike broke the news to Daphne that her father had come to the coffee shop to see her while she was out, he had obviously expected her to be pleased. But she wasn't pleased. The last person she wanted to see was her father; she didn't want him anywhere near her.

'I couldn't handle it,' she told Des that evening. 'Honestly. My stomach has been in knots ever since Mike mentioned it.'

'You still haven't told me why you left home, you know.'

'I've been trying to forget it myself.'

'I'd still like to know why you're so worked up about seeing your father again.'

Daphne hesitated; the last thing she wanted to do was revive it all again. 'Let's just say that my parents were responsible for the death of someone I cared about very deeply,' she said with feeling, 'and I'll never forgive them for it.' Not wishing to discuss the matter any further, she walked away to find something to do that would take her mind off her father who, if she could help it, was not about to re-enter her life.

It was Madge Mitchell who let slip the fact that Des and Daphne's father had been drinking together the following afternoon in the Waterhole Bar of Lassiter's Hotel. 'How long is your father staying?' she asked after she had given her order in the coffee shop.

'What?' Daphne stared at her.

Madge chuckled softly. 'You didn't tell us what a fine, distinguished-looking man he is.'

120

'What are you talking about?' Daphne demanded in an icy tone.

'Your father. He was in the Waterhole earlier, having a drink with Des.'

Daphne's face tightened with suppressed rage. So that was it. A conspiracy. The two of them getting chummy in the Waterhole Bar. Well, that was something Daphne had to put a stop to right there and then. Dropping everything, she marched with grim determination to the bank. Des was on the telephone as she burst into his office. 'You rat,' she cried.

Des gave her a startled look then covered the mouthpiece of the receiver with his hand. 'Please, Daph,' he whispered urgently. 'I'm on the phone.'

'You'll be on the floor by the time I've finished with you,' Daphne snarled.

Keeping a wary eye on his infuriated spouse, Des spoke briefly into the mouthpiece, apologised and promised to call back. He replaced the receiver. 'Daph, I tried. I was going to call.'

'I can't believe you would do something like that.'

'All I did was have a drink with him.'

'You know the way I feel about him.'

'Look, he walked into the bank,' Des said nervously. 'He asked me if we could have a talk.' He gave a helpless shrug. 'What was I supposed to say?'

'You were supposed to say no.'

'Oh, come on, Daph . . .'

'You're supposed to be my husband,' Daphne cried angrily. 'And I had this funny feeling that being my husband meant that you would be on my side—that my enemies would be your enemies.'

'But, Daph, he's not your enemy.'

'As far as I'm concerned, he is.'

'All he wants is a chance to make up with you.'

'I gave him fifteen years. How much more of a chance does he want?'

'Just one more.'

'I'm not interested,' Daphne snapped. 'I don't want anything to do with him.' She glared at her husband, the turncoat. 'And if you've got any consideration for the way I feel, you won't see him either.'

'Yeah . . . um . . . it's not quite that simple,' Des told her awkwardly.

'Why?' Daphne's nerve-ends were straining; she could tell by his guilty expression that he had gone and done something stupid. '*What* have you done?'

'I invited him round to our place.'

She might have known. Treachery of the first order. People were shot for less. 'Well, you can just to and uninvite him.'

'I can't do that.'

'Okay, all right.' The damage had been done; her father had been invited. 'You have him round then,' she said tightly. 'Boys together, and I hope you enjoy yourself— because I won't be there.' She gave him another withering look which seemed to make him shrink even further down behind his desk, then stormed out of the office.

Back at the coffee shop, Mike was seated at one of the tables, working on an essay. Still furious with Des, Daphne made a lot of noise as she cleared the other tables. When Mike glanced up at her with a frown, she rounded on him. 'If you don't like the noise, you can always go somewhere else.'

Mike looked hurt. 'I didn't say a word, did I?'

'You didn't have to.'

The door opened. 'Yoo-hoo, Daphne,' a voice called sweetly.

'Oh no,' Daphne groaned as her mother-in-law swept boldly into the coffee shop. 'Not again.'

It was too late for Daphne to escape; she had already been spotted. 'I've made a nice cream sponge for dessert,' Eileen announced.

'What?' Then, with a wince, Daphne remembered. Eileen was coming home for dinner that night. 'Oh, tonight . . .'

'I could do the main course, too, if you like,' Eileen prattled on happily. 'I mean, after all, it's not fair that you

122

should have to work here all day then go home and cook for us.' Her eyes dropped to Daphne's stomach. 'Especially in your condition,' she added significantly.

Daphne had quite forgotten that Eileen was coming for dinner. 'Look, Eileen,' she said apologetically, 'we'll have to call it off for tonight.'

'But we can't.' Eileen looked shocked. 'I've already made the cream sponge.'

'I'm sorry, but it wouldn't be a good night for you to come around.'

'But I've got the cream and made a passionfruit topping.'

Daphne was beginning to lose her patience. 'It's off,' she said firmly. 'All right? That's it. Final.'

'Well . . .' Eileen was becoming quite huffy. 'At least I deserve an explanation.'

Daphne picked up the tray from the table and headed for the kitchen. 'Then I suggest you ask your son,' she said coldly.

She was determined not to be in the house when her father arrived. Des and Mike had had their dinner. She was ready to go out. 'Daph, can't you just give him five minutes?' Des pleaded with her.

'No, Des,' she said with finality. 'Not even one minute.'

Mike pushed his chair back from the table and stood up. 'I'd better get going,' he said. 'I'm taking Jane to the pictures.'

Des nodded to him. 'Okay, mate. Enjoy yourself.'

'It looks like you're on your own,' Daphne told Des after Mike had gone.

She was heading for the front door when to her horror the doorbell sounded. She froze. It had to be her father. She swung back to Des. 'You invited him, you answer it.'

She was making for the back door when Des intercepted her and lightly grabbed her arm. 'Give him a chance, Daph,' he urged. 'Just listen to what he has to say.'

Daphne pulled away from him. 'He had all the chances he needed,' she said tautly. 'Years ago. Now I've got *nothing* to say to him.'

The doorbell sounded again. Des moved to answer it.

Daphne continued towards the back door. She was just about to open it when, to her surprise, she heard Eileen's voice in the hall. Her hand fell away from the door handle. She turned back to the living room just as Eileen scuttled in with a covered plate. 'What are you doing here, Eileen?' she demanded.

'I've come to welcome your father to Ramsay Street. As a member of the family, he deserves at least a little courtesy.'

Daphne was most annoyed that Des's mother should have turned up with her sponge cake after Daphne had specifically told her not to come. She had obviously gone to see Des in the bank immediately after leaving the coffee shop. Des would have told her about Daphne's problem with her father. 'Des, will you *please* tell your mother to mind her own business for once.'

Des looked unhappily at his mother. 'Mum, would you please . . .'

Eileen ignored him. 'You should at least talk to him,' she said reproachfully to Daphne. 'Show him the respect he deserves.'

'You and Des show him all the respect you like,' Daphne said angrily as she turned once again to the door. 'I'm going.'

'Where are you going?' Des queried.

'Out.' She closed the door firmly behind her.

She didn't go far; she went next door where the Robinsons were still having their dinner. 'I was hoping you wouldn't mind some company for a few hours,' she said to Helen Daniels. 'I'm . . . well . . . I'm at a bit of a loose end.'

'Of course not,' Helen assured her. 'You're welcome to stay as long as you like.'

Jim Robinson looked shrewdly up at Daphne from his lamb chop. 'You and Des haven't had a fight, have you?' he asked.

'Oh no,' Daphne replied quickly. 'Nothing like that, really. I just needed to get out for a while.'

'Well, you stay as long as you like,' Helen said with a smile. 'Whatever the problem is.'

And it was this problem she eventually found herself discussing with Helen and Jim. Her relationship with her father—she felt she did need to talk about it with someone, if only to get it into some sort of perspective in her own mind. 'Dad was away so often that we never had much of a chance to develop a normal relationship,' she was saying to Jim as Helen came in from the kitchen with the freshly brewed coffee. 'And then, with what happened to Matt . . .' she sighed unhappily. 'I gave up altogether.'

Helen placed the tray on the table in front of them. 'Perhaps that's understandable,' she said sympathetically. 'After what you've told us.'

'Then again,' Jim said with a thoughtful frown, 'maybe you're doing more harm than good by refusing to see him. I mean, you're not fifteen any more, are you?'

Helen gave him a stern look. 'She's well aware of that, Jim,' she said crisply, then turned back to Daphne. 'I realise how badly you were hurt by what your father did, but you can't run away forever. And it seems, from what you've told us, he's determined to see you.'

Daphne could see what they were both driving at. 'I guess I am being a bit of an ostrich,' she said with a wan smile. 'Sticking my head in the sand. But I can't even bear the thought of being in the same room as him.'

'I always thought you were made of sterner stuff than that, Daphne,' Jim said in mild reproach. 'You're not the type to run away. From anyone.'

No, she wasn't. When there were things that needed to be faced . . . Of course, Jim was right. 'And that's exactly what I'm doing, isn't it?' she said. 'Exactly what I have always told other people not to do.' Gripped by a new determination, she rose to her feet. 'Well, he hasn't got the better of me yet. If it's a confrontation he wants, then that's what he can have.'

Her father was just leaving when she arrived back at the house. They stood up at the front door, staring at each other for a long, tense moment before Des and Eileen bustled them back inside. Daphne was defiant; she was determined to give nothing away; she wouldn't allow him to see how apprehensive she was at this meeting after so many years.

The tension in the room was palpable. Obviously determined to be instrumental in the reconciliation between father and daughter, Eileen was doing her best to ease it. She began to fuss. She talked about the weather. Autumn was her favourite time of the year, she said. Allen Lawrence didn't seem to be particularly interested. Des tried to draw her away so that Daphne could be alone with her father.

'Why don't we take the coffee out the back?' he suggested. 'I mean, we've hardly used that outdoor furniture you gave us.'

'Nonsense, Desmond. It's freezing out there.'

'You were just saying how much you like this time of the year,' Des said in exasperation. 'Now come on, Mum. Why don't we leave Daphne to talk to her father?'

'There's no need for that,' Daphne said flatly. 'Anything I say to him can be said in front of you and Eileen.' Eileen gave her son a satisfied smile as they went out to the kitchen to prepare the coffee. Daphne glanced coldly at her father who, apart from being a little greyer, hadn't changed much over the years. 'All right, I'm here now. What do you want?'

Allen Lawrence was looking uncomfortable in the easy chair opposite her. 'Look, Daphne . . . I know it must be something of a shock, my turning up like this. But I did hope . . . after all this time . . . that we could settle our differences.'

'Some hope,' Daphne said with a grimace of distaste.

Allen Lawrence still tried to get through to his daughter. 'I realise . . . business commitments being what they are . . . well, I wasn't always the father you wanted me to be.'

'Oh yes.' Daphne allowed her bitterness to show. 'We mustn't let the business down, must we? Look,' she went on after a brief pause, 'why don't you just give up? This is impossible. We don't even *like* each other as people.'

126

'But that could change . . . if we tried.'

Daphne shook her head. 'No, it couldn't.'

'Why not?'

'Because after all that has happened, I'm incapable of liking you.'

Des brought the coffee cups in from the kitchen. Eileen followed him with the coffee pot. 'More coffee?' Des asked.

'He won't be staying,' Daphne said with a curt nod towards her father, 'so there's no need.'

'Oh fiddle faddle,' Eileen exclaimed. 'You must have so much family chit-chat to catch up on.'

Daphne glared at Des who seemed to be incapable of shutting this woman up. 'Okay,' she said with heavy sarcasm to her father. 'How's Mum?'

Allen Lawrence's reply was quite matter-of-fact. 'She left me three years ago. She married a stockbroker.'

'Finally wised up to you, did she?'

'Daphne,' Eileen cried out in alarm. 'I'm surprised at you.'

Daphne was about to snap back at her when Des intervened. 'Come on, Mum,' he said. 'I'd better take you home.'

But Eileen was having none of that. 'Oh no, Desmond,' she said, shaking off the hand he had placed on her arm. 'I can see my calming influence is definitely needed around here at the moment.'

The situation didn't improve. Allen Lawrence tried to make conversation, but Daphne didn't make it easy for him. 'So despite everything for the past ten years,' he said, rounding off a brief summary of his career to date, 'the sales have sky-rocketed. The business has made me quite a wealthy man, but . . .' he spread his hands in a gesture of uncertainty . . . 'I sometimes wonder what it has all been for.'

Daphne had heard enough. 'For you. Who else?'

'That's not true, Daphne.' Allen Lawrence shook his head sorrowfully. 'I did it for all of us. I wanted my daughter . . . my little girl to have the best of everything. But I suppose I *was* too busy to give her what she really needed . . . love, attention.' He stared at the daughter who had been so neglected all those years ago. 'And I intend to make up for it,' he promised.

Eileen, who had been hanging onto every word, decided it was a good moment to act as peacemaker. 'Of course you do,' she said, then smiled at Daphne. 'You understand that now, don't you, Daphne?'

'I'll *never* understand,' Daphne said coldly. 'And I'll *never* forgive him.'

'But, Daphne.' Eileen tried to make her see reason. 'We parents are only human, too. Now, whatever you imagine your father did to you . . .'

'I didn't imagine anything,' Daphne snapped at her. 'If I was the only one who had suffered, then maybe I *could* forgive and forget. But there was someone else . . . someone I loved very much.' She turned back to her father. 'You wanted the best of everything for me. But Matt just didn't fit into your high expectations, did he?'

Allen Lawrence shifted uncomfortably on his chair. 'That was a long time ago,' he murmured. 'And I'm sure Des doesn't want to hear about your old boyfriends.'

'Then it's about time he did,' Daphne said tersely. 'You, too, Eileen.'

'What happened to the boy was an accident,' her father protested.

'And you caused the accident.' She looked across at Des and Eileen who were beginning to look uneasy. 'Matt Foster was my first real boyfriend,' she explained. 'I was only fifteen, but I loved him. I really loved him. Apart from the housekeeper, he was the only person who ever showed me any affection.'

'Daphne . . .' Allen Lawrence gestured unhappily. 'I'm sure there's no point . . .'

'But he wasn't from the right area,' Daphne went on, vehemently overriding him. 'And his parents were dirt as far as my family was concerned. But I didn't give a damn.' The bitter memories were flooding back to her. With some difficulty, she kept her voice even. 'Mum and Dad tried everything they could to stop me seeing him, but I wasn't letting go. Not for anything. So they hatched a little plot. They managed to get me out of the way long enough to tell Matt that I had made a mistake, that I didn't really love him. Poor Matt . . .' She sighed deeply. 'He cared as much about me as I cared about him. He went out and got drunk. And, on the way home, he crashed his car.' It wasn't easy for her; she was reliving something she had tried so hard to put out of her mind. Once again, she could see Matt's face, hear his voice. It was all so vivid. 'He was hurt very badly,' she continued. 'He kept calling for me. His mother phoned the house to try and get me to go to the hospital. Dad took the message. The next day I read about Matt's death in the newspaper.' She shook her head slowly. 'Maybe some people could forgive their parents for that. But I can't.'

The silence in the room was brief but intense. Crossing to her, Des took Daphne's hand and held it. Eileen rose to her feet. 'Ah . . . in the circumstances,' she said with some awkwardness, 'I think I had better be going. Des, will you drive me home, please.'

Des looked uncertainly at Daphne. 'Go on,' she said quietly. 'I'll be all right.'

'I won't be long.'

Daphne turned back to her father. 'I think it's time you went, too,' she said.

But he didn't leave immediately. 'You rather enjoyed your little scene, didn't you?' he said after Des and Eileen had gone and Daphne was finding some relief for her frustration by tidying up the room. 'Putting me in my place for the benefit of your mother-in-law, and Des.'

'It was no one's fault but your own,' Daphne coldly informed him. 'Playing the helpless, neglected father—what did you expect?'

'I expected to try and repair the damage.' He looked up at her earnestly. 'I do care, you know. You're my daughter, my only child.'

'So?' Daphne's expression was stony. 'What has that *ever* meant to you?' she demanded. 'You may think you spoilt me as a child, but you never gave me any of the things I really needed. And all it would have cost you was your precious time.'

'Look, Daphne, can't you see that the business with Matt . . . the mistake that was made . . . it was only because we were worried about you. Your mother and I saved you from doing something you would have regretted for the rest of your life. The simple fact is, that boy was not able to provide for you.' He included the room in a sweeping gesture. 'You certainly wouldn't have had all this comfort you have now. Like it nor not, I *was* trying to protect you.'

'Why?' Daphne wanted to know. 'You've only ever thought of me as a possession. You never loved me, and I don't think you ever loved Mum.' She paused briefly. 'You and I have a very different idea of what that word means. Now . . .' she pointed to the door; enough had been said, and there was no point in carrying it on any further. 'Would you please leave. I want to be left alone. You can see yourself out.'

'Fair enough.' At the front door, Allen Lawrence stopped and turned back to face her. 'But I'll be back,' he said quietly, but with determination. 'I didn't get to where I am now by being a quitter.'

He was up to something—Daphne was quite certain of it, and she wished she knew what it was. There just had to be a reason behind this sudden urge to make amends. It worried her very much.

He had warned her he wouldn't give up. It seemed he had planned a deliberate campaign to win her over. First, there were the flowers, then a day later, the diamond bracelet that must have cost a small fortune. 'Oh, why won't he leave me alone,' Daphne wailed, slamming shut the box in which the bracelet nestled and throwing it onto the floor.

'Maybe he's trying to show you something,' Des suggested.

'What?'

'That he loves you. And needs you.'

Daphne pulled angrily away from him. 'I don't want to have anything to do with him,' she cried. 'And I'll have to

130

tell him that face to face to get it through his thick skull—
and that's what I will do.'

'Don't you think you're being a bit hard on him?' Des
queried. 'It was just a present.'

'It's not a present. It's a bribe.'

'It's probably his way of making it up to you.'

'More like his way of trying to buy me back,' Daphne
retorted. 'I know him.' She moved towards the front door.
'Come on. You can drive me to his place. I'm too angry to
drive myself. I would only be a menace on the road.'

Des hung back. 'Why do you want to go there now?'

Daphne had picked up the present from the floor. 'To
return this,' she said, brandishing it. 'If he thinks he can
buy me over with expensive jewellery, he's got another
think coming.'

'No,' Des said as she turned once more for the door.
'Come and sit down here for a moment,' he invited, taking
her arm and leading her back into the living room. He sat
down beside her on the couch. 'I just want you to make
sure you know what you're doing before you make any big
decisions.'

'I made my decisions years ago,' she curtly reminded
him. 'I didn't want to have anything to do with him then,
and I don't want to have anything to do with him now.'

'But he's making such an effort,' Des gently pointed out
to her. 'He obviously wants to be near you.'

Daphne laughed shortly. 'That'll be the day.'

'Yeah . . . well . . . at least you've got a choice.' Des was
suddenly thoughtful. 'I haven't seen my own father since I
was twelve,' he went on quietly. 'I don't know where he
is. To all intents and purposes, I don't have one.'

'Good,' Daphne said. 'You can have mine, if you like.'

'Now you're being really silly.'

Daphne patted his hand. 'Look, Des, I understand.
You've missed having a father. But, really, as far as mine
is concerned . . . I'd be better off without him.'

'How can you be sure?' Des asked her. 'I mean, what
would happen if he died, or something, and you were still
fighting with him?'

'It wouldn't make any difference,' she assured him with a definite shake of her head. 'You don't know him, Des.'

'Eight years is a long time, Daph,' Des reminded her. 'Maybe you don't know him yourself any more.'

But no matter how hard he tried to persuade her, Daphne wouldn't be swayed. She still intended to see her father and return his present. In the end, Des agreed to drive her to her father's house.

He waited in the car while she walked up the path to the front door. She looked around her, at the trees, the gently sloping lawns and the flowerbeds. Nothing had changed; it wouldn't have been too difficult for her to imagine that she hadn't been away for so many years. Yes, it took her back. She was a young girl again, a kid, and her father was calling to her. She heard his voice; he was telling her something; he was ordering her to remain in her room because there were people coming over for drinks. She shook her head quickly to banish the memory.

'Can't you realise that what I'm trying to do—for what it's worth—is to say that I'm sorry?'

They were sitting on the terrace. Now that she was back in these old, too familiar surroundings, Daphne wasn't feeling quite so certain about her reactions to her father any more, particularly now that he was trying to tell her that he was sorry. He had seen her from the terrace, and calling her name, smiling in a most friendly way, had hurried towards her. She had thrust his present at him. He had asked her to stay; there were things he wanted to tell her.

'I don't know what to think any more. Except that it won't work. It never has, and it never will.'

'But, Daphne, for God's sake . . . You must at least give me the chance. I'm not looking forward to growing old . . . and lonely.'

Daphne looked at him, and suddenly it seemed to her that he had aged a little; he was looking quite tired. Emotional blackmail, she told herself; that was what he was trying to pull. But all the same . . .

Allen Lawrence fetched Des from the car. When they were seated again on the terrace, he said, as if a thought had just struck him, 'Oh, by the way, I had lunch with my solicitor yesterday. He has agreed to look into the matter of setting up a trust fund for my future grandchild.'

Daphne looked at him with sudden suspicion. 'How did you know I was pregnant.'

Her father seemed to hesitate for a moment before indicating the maternity dress Daphne was wearing. 'It's rather obvious, isn't it?' To Daphne, he sounded a little evasive.

'No, it isn't. I'm hardly showing. And this is the first time I have worn a maternity dress.' She glanced across at Des. 'You didn't say anything, did you?'

'I can't recall who told me,' Allen Lawrence said as Des shook his head. 'It was probably that young fellow at the coffee shop when I called in to see you.'

'Probably.' Des smiled at him. 'Mike's more excited about the baby than we are. More or less,' he added when Daphne frowned at him.

'Anyway . . .' Allen Lawrence picked up from where he had been interrupted. 'I intend to see that this child will be well looked after. Everything that is needed . . . I'll give it to him.'

'It just might be a girl,' Daphne pointed out to him.

'Oh, the odds are that it will be a boy.' Allen Lawrence sounded quite confident about that. 'The Lawrence women are noted for providing sons.' He smiled at Daphne. 'You were the only exception.'

'And don't I know it,' Daphne said bitterly. He had always wanted a boy; he had set his heart on it. She rose to her feet. 'Come on, Des. I think we should be going. I've got a few more things to do.'

'Yeah . . . well . . .' Des gave Allen Lawrence an embarrassed smile. 'Well, thanks for having us,' he said as he pushed himself up out of the chair. 'And we'll see you again soon, I hope.'

'I hope so, too,' Allen Lawrence said. 'And the sooner the better.' He turned to Daphne. 'You look after yourself now.'

'Goodbye,' Daphne said.

They were walking back along the path when Allen

Lawrence caught up with them. 'I think you've forgotten something,' he said, holding out the jewellery box Daphne had so abruptly returned to him.

She stared at the box, then at her father. 'I think we should just take it step by step,' she said evenly. She took a few steps along the path. Des hurried after her.

'Daph . . .'

She stopped and looked back at her father who was watching her with an expression of appeal in his eyes. Perhaps she was being too hard on him, she thought; perhaps he did deserve another chance. She didn't know; she wasn't sure about anything any more. She took a chance; she did feel sorry for him. She took a deep breath, and hoped she wouldn't regret what she was about to do.

'Look, Dad, why don't you come to lunch tomorrow?' she invited him. 'Des's mother will be there.'

Allen Lawrence nodded. 'Yes, I'd like that.'

'All right. We'll see you then.'

When Mike told her that he was quite positive that he hadn't mentioned the subject of her pregnancy to her father who, he was quite sure had brought up the matter himself, Daphne became even more suspicious. She had an idea. 'Des, I need your help,' she said.

'Sure. What then?'

'I want you to back me up tomorrow when he comes to lunch. Just go along with everything I say.'

'Sounds easy enough. Why?'

'I hope I'm wrong,' Daphne said thoughtfully, 'but I've got an awful sneaking suspicion—and there's only one way to make sure. You'll just have to trust me.'

They were in the kitchen, preparing dinner. Des was peeling potatoes. 'Seems like a pretty lonely bloke to me,' he observed. 'Perhaps you're misjudging him.'

'Perhaps I am,' Daphne said. 'I'll find out tomorrow, won't I?'

'I still don't see why you have to set a trap for him,' Des said. 'He just wants to get back together with you again—that's the way I see it.'

But Des didn't know her father. 'Things are never that

134

simple with him, Des. I remember Mum saying once that he never did anything without an ulterior motive.' She sighed as she stirred the gravy. 'She was right.' She became aware that Des was regarding her rather narrowly. 'What's wrong?'

'It's just that I'm not sure that I like it,' he said in a quiet voice, 'when you're so . . . calculating and suspicious like this.'

Daphne was a little hurt by his attitude. 'Des, I've had a grudge against my father for a long time, she said crisply. 'And I'm willing to let that go. But I'm not going to lower all my defences and risk getting hurt again. I did that too many times as a child. This time, I'm keeping my guard up until I'm absolutely sure.'

'All right.' Des picked up another potato. 'I just hope your suspicions prove wrong.'

'So do I,' Daphne said with no certainty at all that they would be. 'So do I.'

Eileen Clarke arrived quite early the following morning to help Daphne prepare the lunch. She seemed quite pleased when Daphne told her that her father would be joining them. 'I'm so glad that you've found it in your heart to let bygones be bygones,' she said with a smile.

Daphne was preparing a roast for lunch. When he arrived, bearing a huge bunch of flowers, Allen Lawrence sniffed the air appreciatively. 'I'm really looking forward to a family Sunday lunch,' he said. 'It's been such a long time since I've had one.'

Daphne gave him a sharp look. 'As far as I remember, you were always too busy playing golf to bother about having lunch with Mum and me.'

As Allen began to look uneasy, Des stepped in quickly to cover the threatening breach in this supposedly smooth family reunion that had hardly even begun. 'A golfer, are you, Allen?' he asked. 'I've sometimes thought about taking it up myself.'

'Really?' Allen Lawrence looked at him with interest. 'I can get you into a very good club, if you like.'

During lunch, Eileen chatted away quite happily, but

135

Daphne hardly touched her food. 'What's the matter, dear?' Eileen queried when she finally noticed this. 'Aren't you feeling well?'

Daphne was feeling tense. 'I'm not very hungry,' she murmured.

'But you must eat up,' Eileen insisted. 'You're eating for two now, you know.'

'That's right.' Allen Lawrence smiled across the table at his daughter. 'We want a big healthy boy, don't we?'

Now it was the moment for Daphne to spring her trap. With a quick glance at Des, she said, 'I know you're very keen that it should be a boy. But there's something you should know. I had an ultra-sound done about a week or so ago. The baby is a girl.'

Allen Lawrence slowly lowered his fork and stared at Daphne. 'Why didn't you tell me?' Eileen demanded. 'How could you *do* something like this, and keep me in the dark?' She was clearly upset by the news. She turned reproachfully to her son. 'Des, I am your mother. Don't you think it's important that I should know something like this? I mean, I could have been knitting things in pink instead of . . .'

'We didn't intend to tell anyone,' Daphne interrupted her. 'But as my father seemed so positive that it would be a boy, I thought I should set the matter straight.'

'Well, we knew it was a possibility,' Allen Lawrence said grudgingly. 'We all knew that. Better luck next time.'

'We don't consider it bad luck at all, Allen.' Des was managing to keep his voice light. 'We're happy to be having a little girl.' He reached for Daphne's hand.

'Yes, well . . .' Eileen was considering the new possibilities with which she had been faced. 'A little girl *would* be nice . . .'

Daphne looked across at her father. 'It won't upset your plans, will it?' she asked. 'About the trust fund, I mean. It will be wonderful to know that she has that behind her for her education . . .'

Allen Lawrence frowned at her. 'Oh, we don't need to spend that sort of money on a girl's education,' he muttered. 'I mean, it's hardly the same as it is for a boy.'

Daphne was appalled; the man was straight out of the Middle Ages. 'Oh . . . you know . . . these days,' Des said with a nervous smile. 'Equal opportunity and all that.'

Allen's disappointment was giving way to annoyance. 'Equal opportunity?' He shook his head grimly. 'Now, don't start me on that. Ridiculous idea.'

Des leaned forward; he spoke very deliberately. 'I'm not sure what you're saying here, Allen. But am I to understand that you *won't* be setting up a trust fund if the child is a girl?'

'Look . . .' Allen Lawrence gestured in exasperation. The food on the plate in front of him was forgotten. 'The world is run by men. It always has been. Women may not like the fact, but it's true. It's nature's way.' He shook his head again. 'To set up a trust fund like that for a girl would simply be a waste of money.'

Eileen was showing her astonishment, but Daphne wasn't surprised at all. This was her father of old; she knew him very well. She had been right in her suspicions, and she wished she hadn't been. The old hurts flooded back into her, the anger . . . Abruptly, she pushed back her chair and stood up. She moved away from the table, wanting to distance herself from her father as far as she could. 'That's what you've always thought, isn't it?' she cried bitterly. 'Boys are important, and girls are not.'

'I never said that . . .'

'But you have always thought it. You have always shown it in the way you treated me.'

Allen tried desperately to justify himself, to placate Daphne's rising anger. 'Look, all I'm saying is that as a man who has been successful in business, I'm looking for a male heir.' With hands outspread, he appealed to them all. 'That's not so strange, is it?'

'And what am *I* supposed to be?' Daphne cried. 'A brood mare? Well . . .' she smiled tightly. 'I've got news for you. I didn't have an ultra-sound. We don't know what the baby is. It might be a boy—or a girl. But Des and I don't care. We'll love it, whatever it is.'

137

'You lied to me.' Allen Lawrence stared at her in bewilderment. 'Why?'

'Because I didn't think you had changed so much,' Daphne replied. 'And I was right. You know . . .' Her laugh was a little unsteady and totally lacking in mirth. 'You could have fooled me completely, if you had said only one thing. If you had said "I love you, Daphne", I would have fallen hook, line and sinker. Because those are the words I have always wanted to hear. But you . . .' her voice rose until it had become quite shrill . . . 'you don't know the meaning of them, do you?'

The lunch was ruined. Allen was also on his feet. He shouted back at his daughter. 'I came here for a simple family lunch. I didn't expect to be the butt of some idiotic game.'

Des was between them. 'I wasn't happy with what Daphne intended to do,' he said to Allen. 'I thought she was being overly suspicious. Now I know she was right.'

Allen glared furiously at him. 'She's nothing but the stupid, useless female that she always was, and always will be.'

Des advanced on him with threatening intent. 'I will *not* have Daphne insulted,' he growled. He pointed to the door. 'I suggest you get out right now.'

'You are fools, you know.' Allen Lawrence looked at them all in turn. 'If you ever *do* have a son,' he said, 'he's not going to thank you for throwing away the opportunity for him to become a wealthy man. You just bear that in mind.'

Then he was gone. Daphne was close to tears. She gave another shaky laugh. Des placed his arm around her. 'I love you, Daphne,' he said quietly.

'Oh, Des . . .' She clung to him tightly, desperately. She needed him so much.

Ten

Some people seemed to have a habit of popping up out of the past and throwing a spanner in the works. Gail Lewis's ex-husband was one such individual. 'What is he after? That's what I want to know.'

'Maybe he's still in love with you,' Paul suggested.

Gail dismissed this out of hand. 'No way. He doesn't know what love is. Not real love, anyway.'

Gail had been worrying about it ever since that totally unexpected encounter at Lassiter's Hotel where she and Paul had been discussing the Udugawa deal over dinner. Jeremy Lord had been quite insistent that she have lunch with him the following day; there were things they needed to talk about, he had said. He had tried to buy them a drink, but Gail had refused outright. 'He's really got you wound up, hasn't he?' Paul observed.

'But who does he think he is? Barging in like that? Just when I was beginning to forget him, and . . . everything was going so well. Oh . . .' She sat unhappily in Paul's office and twisted her fingers together. 'I should have known.' She sighed deeply. 'What *does* he want?'

Paul was unable to offer any thoughts about that. 'He said something about unfinished business,' he recalled.

'Yes, but what?'

'I don't know.' Paul shrugged. 'There's always something. Things you wish you had said—or hadn't said, for that matter.'

'I'm sorry, Paul.' Gail gave him a weak smile. 'This is my problem not yours. It's just . . . well, it's my life and I don't want him in it.'

'Then you should tell him that.'

Gail's laugh sounded strained. 'If it was only that simple. The trouble is, Jeremy never takes no for an answer.'

'But if you mean it, he will just have to accept it.'

'You don't know him,' Gail said ruefully, and Paul suddenly realised what the problem really was.

'Perhaps . . .'—he chose his words carefully—'the real problem is that you don't know *how* to say no . . . isn't that it?'

Her quick, startled glance told him he had hit the nail on the head. 'Don't be silly,' she said without conviction. 'I'm just tired, that's all.' She shook her head. 'He doesn't worry me. I can handle him.' Watching her shrewdly, Paul wasn't so sure about that. 'Oh, I'm such an idiot,' Gail said with another forced laugh. 'Here I am . . . Gail Lewis . . . career woman, on top of the world—and then Jeremy Lord walks in with all his old charm . . . and I fall to pieces.' She smiled a little too brightly. 'Dumb, isn't it?'

It didn't take long for Gail to discover just what was behind Jeremy's sudden reappearance on the scene. It was that damned racing car, she told Paul in disgust as she stormed angrily back into the office the following afternoon. He and Gail's father were involved in it together. 'Now they're as thick as thieves,' she exclaimed.

'But cars are Rob's business,' Paul reminded her.

'I know that,' Gail retorted. 'And Dad's a very good motor mechanic, when he puts his mind to it. But this is no ordinary car. It's a jinx, and an obsession. You see, Dad and Trevor Lord—that's Jeremy's father—poured years into it, and every cent they could lay their hands on. When we were kids, we spent hours hanging around the garages and the tracks because that was the only way we ever got to see our fathers.'

Paul still couldn't see what the problem was. 'But lots of guys are fascinated by racing cars. My Dad, for instance . . .'

'But this car is different,' she broke in. 'I told you that. It's trouble. It's dangerous. Trevor Lord knew that, but it didn't stop him, even though it was blowing his marriage apart. He wouldn't listen to his wife. He was starting to win races, and that was all he cared about. Then . . .' some of the anger went out of her voice . . . 'there was a dreadful crash . . . and he was killed instantly.'

'Then why has the car just suddenly reappeared?' Paul wanted to know.

'Somehow Jeremy got his hands on it,' she replied, 'and now the whole nightmare is starting all over again.'

'Yes, but I mean, if he wants Rob to work on it . . .'

'Weren't you listening?' she snapped at him. 'Haven't you heard a single word of what I have just said?' She gestured impatiently. 'That car is a killer—and Dad is just as obsessed with it as he was the first day Trevor Lord came into our lives.'

For the next couple of days, Paul was involved in discussions with Mr Udugawa, a small and softly spoken Japanese businessman. These discussions held out enormous possibilities for the Daniels Corporation as Mr Udugawa was anxious to extend the holdings of his company to Australia, and the Daniels Corporation, the Australian end of which was Paul's responsibility, could well find itself in an excellent position to handle the Japanese company's investments—if Paul played his cards right. There was one small hitch, however, as he soon discovered in the course of those discussions, as well as on the couple of occasions when he and Gail had taken Mr Udugawa to dinner, and that was that the Japanese businessman had somehow formed the impression that Paul and Gail were engaged to be married. Mr Udugawa had let it be known in many small ways, and possibly in others that were more obscurely oriental, that he approved, that he regarded Paul and Gail as a fine looking couple, and intimated that marriage was something he held in high esteem as a settled state that could offer that desired reliability of which, in all his dealings, particularly with regard to future partnerships, he insisted on taking account. In other words—as Paul understood it— the chances of the Daniels Corporation being successful in these negotiations would be greatly enhanced if Mr Udugawa realised he was dealing with a married man, or a man about to be married. It was virtually a condition of the fantastic deal that he had more than hinted was in the offing. So, to make things easier, and remove any doubts from the mind of Mr Udugawa, Paul told him a white lie. He told him that he and Gail were planning to be married in the not too distant future.

Gail was horrified when she learned what Paul had done. 'Paul, how could you?' she exclaimed.

'Well, you've heard him say it. He thinks married men are more stable, more responsible . . .'

'It wasn't too responsible to tell him we're engaged.'

'I don't think it was such a bad idea.' Paul gave her an embarrassed smile. 'I mean, we get along pretty well, don't we?'

'Oh sure. Fine. But that doesn't mean we should get married.'

'Look, Gail . . . we're pretty similar in a lot of ways.'

'Such as?'

Such as? Paul thought for a moment. 'Well, I want to make something of my life,' he said at last. 'I want to get somewhere. I mean, I've never made that a secret, have I?'

'There's nothing wrong with being ambitious,' Gail said flatly.

'Yeah . . . well . . . I have always thought you were fairly much the same. You know . . . keen to make a go of it.'

'You think we'd make a good partnership—is that it?'

'There'd be no drama, nothing to hold you back or tie you down,' Paul promised her. 'We would be able to help each other. As friends.'

Gail faced him squarely. 'Then what you're suggesting is a marriage of convenience. That's what they call it, isn't it?'

'If you like.' Paul shrugged. 'The whole idea is that it should work out to our mutual advantage.'

'Well . . .' Gail smiled slightly. 'I suppose quite a few marriages have been built on less.'

'Yes, and a lot of people become blinded by their emotions,' Paul pointed out to her, 'and end up on the rocks in no time at all. But we both know that.'

'I would still need to give it a lot of thought,' Gail murmured.

He could see that she had given some ground. 'Gail, it would work out perfectly,' he persisted. 'We'd simply be two intelligent people making the wisest possible choice to secure our futures.'

'I think I need some coffee,' Gail said.

When she had made the coffee and they were seated opposite each other again, Paul returned to the attack. 'Look at it as a type of insurance.'

'Against what?'

'Jeremy, for instance. And others like him.'

'Jeremy . . . ?' Gail's expression clouded.

'I know you're worried about the effect he has on you,' Paul told her. 'I can see it. You're edgy.'

'And you think he would back off if I become engaged to you—is that the idea?'

'He and anyone else you didn't want to become involved with.'

'It's a valid point, Paul,' Gail said reflectively. 'But it's a little on the cold-blooded side, isn't it?'

'Most business decisions are.'

'Oh, so you're thinking of a contract?' Gail regarded him levelly. 'Bound by clauses and special conditions instead of vows?'

Paul nodded. 'In a sense—yes. There would be no reason for anyone else to know about it. It would be a private arrangement between the two of us. And if the deal with Mister Udugawa pays off, I might have to expand the entire operation. Then I'll have a ready-made partner.'

'Till death do us part?' Gail's smile was a little cynical. 'You seem to have it all worked out.'

'I wouldn't have it any other way,' Paul assured her.

'Will there be an escape clause?'

'You could always break the contract after a couple of years if you're still not happy with the idea.'

'Divorce, you mean.'

'Why not? And there would be no bitterness. Everything could be divided up quite fairly.'

143

Gail laughed. 'Paul, you're an incurable romantic.'

Paul smiled back at her. 'If you look at it rationally, you'll find it's a very smart move.'

'I'll still need to think it over,' Gail said quietly. 'You know me. I always like to examine the fine print before I come to a decision.'

There was still the problem of Jeremy; Paul knew that Gail still hadn't got him out of her system. He also knew that she was seeing him. While he was quite certain that Jeremy was the one who was taking the initiative there, he was nevertheless a little hurt that Gail didn't seem to be resisting him too strongly. It was true that Jeremy had charm, and was persuasive almost to the point of irresistibility, but Paul thought with disappointment that she could at least have made more of an effort to withstand those qualities.

'He's only using you,' he told Gail. 'And you're far too special . . . Just give yourself some time. Find out how you feel, at least. All I'm asking for is a few weeks. Just let Mister Udugawa think that we're the best thing since raw fish. After that, when the deal is finalised, you can do whatever you want . . .'

Gail looked at him. 'Just until the deal is finalised?'

'That's all I ask. And I promise you won't regret it.'

'Oh . . . why not?' Gail said after a longish pause. 'Nothing else makes much sense at the moment. Why should this be any different?'

The following morning, Jeremy Lord came to see Paul. 'I'll come straight to the point,' he said. 'I won't tolerate Gail being involved in this engagement farce.'

So she had told him about it; it had been one way to force the issue. Paul had been half expecting something like this. 'I don't give a damn whether you tolerate it or not,' he said evenly. 'It's up to Gail, not you. You're ancient history as far as she's concerned.'

'I don't think so,' Jeremy Lord returned with a slow smile. 'I've been seeing her, you know. We've had a long talk. A few wrinkles have been ironed out. Everything is cosy, you might say.'

The man was so assured, so arrogant . . . With an effort, Paul reined in his rising anger. 'I suppose we're all entitled to one weakness,' he remarked.

'Oh, at least,' Jeremy agreed smoothly. 'At least. You and I both have them. Mine is that I desperately need funds for that poor old racing car of mine.'

'I wish you luck then,' Paul said stiffly.

Jeremy ignored him. 'And your weakness is that I have control over Gail,' he said. 'And you know it.'

Paul did know it. 'That's her problem. Her big problem.'

'It's yours, actually,' Jeremy informed him. 'You need Gail to impress your Japanese friend . . . what's his name? Um . . . Mister Udugawa, isn't it?'

Paul tried to bluff him. 'I can always tell him that Gail broke off the engagement. He'll understand.'

'Perhaps.' Jeremy shrugged carelessly. 'They're very honourable people, the Japanese. They have a high regard for family and fair play.'

Paul stared at him. 'Is that all?' he asked in an icy tone.

'No, it isn't.' Jeremy shook his head. 'I have a proposition to make to you.'

Paul was suddenly wary. 'Such as?'

'If you would kindly agree to help me out with funds for my racing car—a sponsorship, say—then *I* will agree that it probably won't be necessary for me to tell Mister Udugawa what a devious businessman you have been.'

'You wouldn't dare.'

'Try me.' Jeremy coolly returned his stare of disbelief.

Seething with indignation, Paul sprang up from behind his desk. 'That's blackmail,' he cried, striding across to the door and wrenching it open. 'The police would agree with me. Now get out.'

Jeremy Lord was not looking quite so composed as before. 'The way I see it, we were just having a friendly chat about our problems,' he said.

'You threatened me for money.'

'Oh . . .' Jeremy spread his hands in a gesture that called for understanding. 'You misunderstand me completely. I was appalled at the way you were using my ex-wife, and I thought I should tell the nice Japanese man that he was being conned. As for the money . . . , we were just discussing the possibility of a sponsorship, that's all.'

'I want you out of this hotel immediately,' Paul ordered angrily. 'I'll have your bill made up.'

Jeremy gave him a half smile. 'Well, that will be the quickest service I've had in this place.'

'Well, you won't have to worry about that any more,' Paul said tautly. 'Because if you are as clever as you think you are, you won't show your face around here again.'

'All right. Have it your own way.' Jeremy stopped in front of him. 'And give my regards to Mister Udugawa.' He smiled quite disarmingly. 'That is, if I don't see him first.'

Paul slammed the door behind him, then had Gail paged to come to his office immediately. When she came, he told her about Jeremy's visit. 'He tried to blackmail me.'

'What?' Gail was clearly shocked.

'Oh yes, he back-pedalled when I threatened to call the police, but it was a classic blackmail attempt as far as I was concerned. You see, he wanted me to pay him some money so he could fix his racing car. Otherwise, he would tell Mister Udugawa about us.'

Gail waved the idea away. 'He wouldn't do anything like that,' she protested. 'He's a frustrated racing-car driver, not an extortionist.'

'I have ordered him out of the hotel,' Paul told her. 'If it wasn't for you, I would have rung the police.' His voice softened. 'Oh Gail, can't you see what he's like? Why do you let him take you for such a fool?'

'Don't call me a fool, Paul,' Gail warned him in a low voice.

'But he's playing on you—can't you see that?'

'That's enough, Paul,' Gail snapped. 'You don't own me. Nobody does . . .'

'Except Jeremy,' Paul muttered.

'And I'll do what I like, *when* I like, and without your assistance, thanks very much. And in case you've forgotten,' she went on vehemently as Paul opened his mouth to protest, 'we're only supposed to appear close for the benefit of Mister Udugawa. And I can't do that if we're fighting. So . . .' she moved back to the door . . . 'I strongly suggest that you stop interfering in my life.' She was storming out of the office, when she decided to loose one last parting shot. 'Or would you call that blackmail?'

When Gail told Paul that she couldn't go through with the engagement, that she wanted him to tell Mr Udugawa the truth, Paul was dismayed. 'Has this got anything to do with what I said about your ex-husband?' he asked.

'Partly,' she replied. 'But it's more to do with the way you think it's your right to interfere in my life.'

'All right, all right,' Paul said quickly. 'I'll back off—okay? After all, you're entitled to find out for yourself. Again,' he added pointedly.

Gail flared up at him. 'That's exactly what I'm talking about,' she said angrily. 'Whether this engagement was a business arrangement or not, you still feel entitled to tell me what to do—and I'm not having it.'

Paul was also becoming angry. 'Yes, and I'm not having you back out on me. This was a business deal—remember?'

'You can just take your business deal, and . . . and . . . oh, to hell with it.'

Mr Udugawa was scheduled to fly out to Alice Springs that morning. On learning that he had already left, Paul was relieved to know that he had a couple of days at least to try and retrieve the situation. 'I just want to know where I stand,' Gail said later that day.

'You made that perfectly clear.'

Gail wasn't seeming so sure of herself now; Paul wondered if she had seen Jeremy in the meantime. 'It wasn't as if the engagement meant anything,' she said. 'It was only a business deal that fell through. But I know what you must be thinking about us working together. So I want to know . . . do I still have the job, or not?'

Ah, so that was it. Paul thought he could let her suffer a little. 'It's not going to be easy. Working together, I mean.'

'Yes,' Gail said in a small voice. 'I know.'

Paul decided it was time to let her off the hook. 'But I have no complaints about your work,' he told her. 'Just as long as that is not affected, the job is still yours.'

'Good.' Gail looked relieved.

'As you said, it was only a business deal . . .'

'Paul, I'm glad you're being reasonable about it.'

'Let's hope Mister Udugawa feels the same way.'

'I've been thinking about that,' Gail said quietly.

Paul nodded. 'Me, too.'

'He's away at the moment,' Gail went on. 'That gives us a few days' breathing space. So . . . when he comes back, why don't we tell him it didn't work out and that I broke it off?' She looked at him hopefully. 'What do you think?'

'So I would look a fool instead of a liar?' Paul queried a little sourly. 'Still, you never know. I mean, he might even feel sorry for me. It could swing things my way even more.' But it wasn't a strong hope.

'Well, let's hope so,' Gail said. 'I wouldn't want you to lose out because of me. But we both know it wouldn't have worked out. Us getting married, I mean.'

'That's not what you thought before Jeremy got to you.'

'Jeremy has got nothing to do with this.'

'Let me give you a piece of advice,' Paul said. 'Just for old time's sake. Don't trust him. That precious ex-husband of yours is so crooked he couldn't lie straight in bed. At least, I've always tried to be honest with you.'

'It's a pity you didn't pay Mister Udugawa the same compliment.'

'I'm only trying to warn you.'

'You can save your breath.'

It was clear to Paul that Gail had come under Jeremy's spell once more; it was the only possible reason for her sudden change of mind. He had worked on her, persuaded her . . . and it was quite probable she had been unable to resist the old charm. He had a hold on her all right. Like a snake with a rabbit, Paul thought bitterly.

When Rob Lewis telephoned him the following morning and told him that there had been an accident, that against his advice Jeremy had taken the racing car out to the track

148

for a test run, that he had lost control and the car had struck the safety fence, flipping right over and killing Jeremy instantly, Paul's first thought was for Gail. He hurried across to the Lewis house where Gail, on first appearance, seemed to be handling the news remarkably well. 'Don't stand in the doorway, Paul,' she greeted him calmly. 'You look like an encyclopaedia salesman.'

Paul didn't know what to say. He tried to put his arm around her to comfort her, but she pulled away. He suggested he call a doctor who might prescribe something to enable her to sleep.

'No, really, I'm fine. I was about to have a good long soak in the bath, but I can do it later.'

'No, you go ahead. If it will help . . .'

After she had gone, Paul mentioned to Rob Lewis how detached his daughter seemed. 'It's been like that ever since it happened,' Rob said unhappily. 'She was there, you know. She saw it happen.' Rob looked pale and stricken. 'Even when the ambulance arrived . . . it was almost as if she wasn't there. It wasn't registering. She hasn't even cried.'

Paul sat down opposite him. 'It could be shock, I suppose.'

Rob was blaming himself for the accident. 'The car wasn't quite right,' he said in a broken voice. 'I told him.'

'But it wasn't your fault.'

Rob stared at him bleakly. 'Well, who else do you blame?' he demanded. 'His old man died exactly the same way . . . and I'm the one who got the car ready. Me.' He tapped himself forcefully on the chest. 'Not some wet-nosed kid who didn't know what he was doing. I'm supposed to be an expert. Expert at what?' he shuddered violently. 'Murder?'

Paul tried to reassure him. 'You did everything you could. Jeremy knew the risks.'

'I still should have stopped him.'

'You can't change it now, Rob,' Paul said quietly.

When he came back that evening to see how she was, Gail had surprising news for him. 'It's a pity you weren't here half an hour ago,' she said in a brittle voice as she showed him into the living room. 'You could have helped me break the bad news to Jeremy's wife.'

'What?' Paul was stunned.

Gail was very tense. 'Yes. Meredith. She has just flown in from Brisbane. She wanted to surprise him.'

'Some surprise.'

'It was. For me.' Paul could see how hurt she was. 'She's upstairs, trying to rest,' Gail said after a brief pause. 'At least . . . I suppose . . . *she's* got some fond memories.'

'Look, Gail,' Paul said with quiet intensity. 'There's no point dwelling on the matter any more. It's over.'

'That's just it, Paul,' Gail said in bitter self-reproach. 'It should have been over when I plucked up the courage to leave him before.' She gave him a small, sad smile. 'The one person I'll never be able to forgive for this mess is myself. I'm a weak fool . . . so why don't you say it?' She eyed him challengingly. 'Say you told me so. Get it over and done with.' Her voice rose. 'Say it.'

'No, Gail, don't . . .'

Gail sighed as the fight suddenly seemed to go out of her. 'He asked me to marry him again, you know. He didn't tell me that he already had a wife.'

'Maybe he was going to divorce her,' Paul suggested.

'Don't make me laugh,' Gail retorted. 'All he wanted was for me not to stop Dad working on his stupid car. Well, he got what he wanted, didn't he? I even lent him money.'

'Gail, you can't change what has happened,' Paul said gently.

'Perhaps not.' Gail shrugged. 'It's over now, it's finished.' Her laugh was a little self-mocking. 'Another lesson learnt.'

By the time Paul had made some coffee, she was much calmer. 'By the way,' he said, 'I'll be in touch with Mister Udugawa first thing in the morning, if it makes you feel any better. I'll tell him the engagement is off.'

Gail frowned slightly. 'Paul, I've been thinking,' she said. 'You don't need to talk to him. I'll be quite happy to go through with the engagement. And . . . if you still want to, we can get married after all.'

150

Paul stared at her in surprise, then quickly shook his head. 'No, no. No. You're still upset. We can talk about it tomorrow.'

'I know what you're thinking,' Gail said calmly. 'But I'm not exactly out of my mind with grief. In fact, I've never felt so sure about anything in my life.'

Paul was flustered. 'Yes, but now is not the time . . .'

'You'd have everything you wanted,' Gail persisted. 'A business partner, a wife to impress clients like Mister Udugawa.'

'But what happens if you change your mind in a year or so?'

'We did discuss contract,' she reminded him. 'But I won't change my mind, Paul,' she said earnestly. 'I married for love once, and I won't risk that again.'

Paul was still not certain. 'You may not think that now . . .'

'They say you always fall in love with the same type,' Gail said. 'There must be millions of Jeremys out there.' She shook her head a little sadly. 'I'm tired of being vulnerable, of being hurt . . .'

Paul understood now what she needed. 'So by marrying me . . . it would be a kind of insurance?'

'The best kind,' Gail answered. 'A cover for life.' She looked up at him expectantly. 'So is it a deal?'

Paul hesitated. He stared at her for a long moment, then smiled and nodded. 'It's a deal,' he said.

Eleven

The woman was actually . . . she was doing . . . merciful heavens, what *was* she doing? Harold Bishop closed his eyes, then opened them again. He saw a tassle that jiggled, a knee and an arm . . . 'That's it!' he cried. It was the last straw. It was the final outrage. He switched off the cassette player. The woman stopped dancing and looked at him blankly. The men in the bar who had been watching this outrageous display—this *lewdness*—began shouting at him. But Harold stood his ground. It was why he was here, in the Waterhole Bar where dear Madge was working behind the counter; he had come to keep an eye on things, which didn't mean keeping an eye on a woman who took off her clothes to a lascivious jungle rhythm. He had come because he had expected the worst; he had heard of these so-called bucks' parties where men drank copious amounts of beer and told ribald stories, along with other undesirable activities, which now included a woman dancing with . . . with . . . *tassles*.

'Hey, what's going on?' someone yelled as the music abruptly stopped.

'Hey, turn it back on again.'

Harold stood there adamantly, with his arms folded. Madge rushed across to him. 'Harold, what do you think you're doing?'

The room was full of smoke and alcohol fumes. 'You can't let this sort of thing go on,' Harold said importantly. 'You'll have the Vice Squad here.'

'Harold, this is a private party. If you don't like it, you can go to the cocktail bar.'

152

Harold didn't like it; he didn't like it a bit. He had sat there in extreme discomfort, casting worried looks at Madge while they told their doubtful stories and guzzled beer, and when Madge had told him they were just having fun, had pointed out to her that he could hardly see where the fun was in telling stories in front of a lady, namely her good self. She had told him that the stories went right over her head, and anyway, she was far too busy to listen. Poor Madge, that she should be subjected to such riotous goings-on. Harold had persevered in his vigil; he had been absolutely tight-lipped about it. Then when the lady customer arrived—or the woman whom he had first thought was a lady customer arrived, he had been pleased at first because he had believed that her welcome presence would quieten this rowdy group. But oh no . . . sequins.

'And leave you here with this bunch of roughnecks?' Never, never; a gentleman had his duty to perform. 'Most certainly not.'

Madge gave a long-suffering sigh. 'All right then,' she said. 'But please don't make any more trouble than there already is.'

She had been surprised to see him when he turned up at the bar. She had offered the opinion that a bucks' night such as the one that was already in progress was hardly his idea of entertainment—and she had been quite right. It wasn't, and that was precisely why he was there; he knew that turns like this could get completely out of hand, and if there was any trouble, he would be there to protect her. Madge hadn't shown too much delight at this, but then she was a woman who didn't always reveal her true feelings.

The woman had covered her nakedness with a coat, and had gone. The drinking continued. There was a lot of shouting and other noisy carryings-on. They sang a suggestive song, and that awful Rob Lewis slipped an arm around Madge's waist. Harold sprang to his feet again. He was a man galvanised by outrage. 'Take your filthy paws off her,' he shouted.

'Harold!' Madge cried warningly.

Harold advanced on the man who was daring to force his

attentions on a family woman. 'How dare you carry on like a bunch of barbarians!' He broke off abruptly when Madge hit him over the head with a tray. 'Ooooooh.' He staggered backwards.

'Harold, get out of here,' Madge ordered him. 'Just go home before you start any more trouble.'

The others were all glaring at him, but Harold wasn't frightened. A woman's honour . . . 'What, and leave you with this bunch of . . .'

'You're the one who needs looking after, Harold,' Madge said sternly. 'Now would you please get out of here.'

She meant business—Harold could see that. It was very odd. He was only trying to help. But if she wanted him to go, and she seemed very determined about it . . . Reluctantly, he left that scene of debauchery a most bewildered man.

He waited for her outside her house. She almost jumped out of her skin when he suddenly loomed out of the darkness as she was letting herself into the house. 'Harold, what are you doing here?'

'I was worried about you.'

'I'm all right, Harold,' she said with laboured patience. 'I told you I would be all right.'

Harold was still puzzled. 'I don't know what you're so upset about. I was only trying to protect you.'

'Be that as it may . . .' Madge regarded him coolly in the light from the front porch . . . 'but I do wish, if you want to play Sir Galahad, that you wouldn't do it at the Waterhole.'

'I'm sorry.'

'It was so embarrassing,' she said unhappily. 'To think I was once their favourite barmaid . . .'

'I said I was sorry.'

'It just wasn't the time or the place, that's all.' Madge opened the front door. 'It's been a long night, and I'm tired. Goodnight, Harold.'

When Madge suggested with some force the following day that Harold go to Rob Lewis's garage and apologise for his unseemly behaviour, it was with the greatest reluctance that he agreed to do so. He did it only for Madge's sake. Rob Lewis was quite affable about it; he said he hardly remembered what had happened the previous night anyway. They shook hands, then Rob Lewis decided to make a peace offering.

Harold frowned disapprovingly at the two bottles Rob had brought out from his workshop. 'Alcohol,' he muttered.

'Apple cider, Harold,' Rob said. 'Brewed from a mountain stream. Terrific stuff. I bottled it myself.'

'Oh, I see.' Harold was heartened by the news that it was only apple cider. 'My Aunt Elizabeth used to bottle fruit in season. She was a whizz with a vacuum seal.'

'Fantastic,' Rob remarked drily.

Harold took the bottles back to Mrs Mangel's house where he rented a room. 'Alcohol, Mister Bishop?' Mrs Mangel sniffed in disapproval when Harold entered the living room with his two bottles.

'Apple cider, Mrs Mangel,' he assured her. 'Fresh as a mountain stream. Brewed locally, you know.'

Mrs Mangel looked impressed. 'Oh, that's a different story,' she said with a smile. 'For a moment there, I thought it was alcohol.'

'Heaven forbid, Mrs Mangel.'

'My mind is set at rest, Mister Bishop.'

They were alone in the house; Jane had gone out for the evening. Harold opened one of the bottles of cider. He was looking forward to a quiet evening. 'Ah . . . now this is what I call luxury,' he said as he handed a glass to Mrs Mangel. 'A night at home, away from the hurly burly. Nothing to do but sit back, put our feet up, sip a nice cool drink, and watch an interesting documentary on television.'

They watched a programme about penguins and sipped their drinks. Harold refilled the glasses. He was enjoying himself; he seemed to be possessing new insights into life in general; in fact, he found himself becoming quite talkative. He sniffed the glass he had just refilled. 'Oh . . . it's got real body,' he pronounced. 'It's got . . . ah, what's the word? Teeth? . . . Yes, it's got teeth.'

'Yes.' Mrs Mangel nodded knowingly. 'Teeth.'

'They don't make apple cider like this any more,' Harold observed. 'And unless I'm very much mistaken, this is . . .' he sniffed the bouquet again . . . 'yes, Jonathons. It's like saying hello to an old friend.'

'We had an apple tree once,' Mrs Mangel recalled rather dreamily. 'Mother would make apple pie.'

'Oh, my word.' Harold was impressed.

'Topped with fresh whipped cream. And the pastry . . .'

'Glorious.'

'One day I shall make you one,' Mrs Mangel promised.

'Marvellous.' Harold beamed at her. What a lovely woman she was. 'Yes, you must.'

'I still have the recipe.'

'Oh . . . will you? Please?'

'I shall.' Mrs Mangel emptied her glass in one gulp.

'It's lovely to know we can still enjoy the simple things in life,' Harold observed as he refilled her glass. 'It's a jungle out there, you know.'

'Oh yes . . .'

'Teeming with misery, desperation, loneliness.' He held his glass up to the light, and squinted at it. 'And we can rejoice in life's pleasures. Like a humble glass of apple cider.'

Mrs Mangel nodded sombrely. 'While others need alcohol.'

Such a shame that others needed the crutch of alcohol. 'Tragic, isn't it?'

'The tool of the devil,' Mrs Mangel said fervently.

'I couldn't agree more.'

They had finished the first bottle, and somehow the room didn't seem to be in quite as sharp a focus as before. By now, Harold was suffused by a soft and gentle glow. 'I look at Ramsay Street, and do you know what I see?'

'Do tell, Mister Bishop.'

'I see a kaleidoscope.' As Mrs Mangel narrowed her eyes in an apparent attempt to share this colourful image, Harold went on. 'It takes all kinds of people to make this world.

156

All kinds. And the young will always make their mistakes. But that's where *we* come in. Us. You and I.'

'Us, Mister Bishop.' Mrs Mangel blinked at him. 'The older generation.'

'You cannot put an . . .'

'. . . old head on young shoulders.'

'Right. Got it in one. Nail on the head.'

'They need us.'

'Exactly.'

'We're like lighthouse keepers,' Harold observed sagely. 'We keep them from straying onto the rocks.' He was warming to the theme; at that moment, he was experiencing a warm and glowing love for the entire human race. 'Especially in these stormy times.'

'Stormy times.'

'Navigate a true course. A steady hand on the helm.'

'They'd be lost without us.'

Harold topped up Mrs Mangel's glass. 'Dashed to pieces.'

'Absolutely dashed.' Mrs Mangel hiccuped.

'Oh dear.' Harold frowned at the empty bottle in his hand. 'Do you think we should open the other one?'

'It is very refreshing,' Mrs Mangel said. 'I haven't felt quite so refreshed in years.'

'Splendid.' Harold clinked his glass lightly against hers. 'To us, Nell.'

'And to all who sail in us . . .' Mrs Mangel looked startled for a moment, then began to titter. Harold also began to laugh.

He opened the second bottle. They were both very relaxed now.

'In my day people really enjoyed themselves,' Mrs Mangel was saying.

'Nowadays, they're in such a rush.'

'Especially young people,' Mrs Mangel concurred. 'They want everything yesterday. They're wishing their lives away.'

'Or . . . or throwing them away.'

'Mmmm . . .'

'Like that young Mike, wanting a motorcycle.'

157

'Oh . . . very dangerous things.'

'And he expects Jane to ride on it.'

'You mustn't let her,' Harold said with fervour. 'She'll get dirty.'

Mrs Mangel shook her head sorrowfully. 'Girls don't seem to care nowadays.'

Harold recalled a detail from his youth. 'You know, my father would wear white cotton gloves to a dance . . . to save the girls' dresses from getting dirty, you know. I did it once.' He sighed. 'I was laughed out of the place.'

'I remember my début,' Mrs Mangel said with a faraway look in her eyes. 'I looked quite beautiful. Some said . . . ravishing.'

'I'm sure you were,' Harold said politely.

'Jane will never make her début.' Mrs Mangel reflected for a moment on her grand-daughter who would never make her début. 'They don't nowadays. It's such a pity. They can't even dance properly.'

'Oh . . .' Harold suddenly slammed the heel of his hand against his forehead. 'I feel so ashamed,' he groaned.

Mrs Mangel gave him a puzzled frown. 'It's hardly your fault . . .'

'My generation's fault, Mrs Mangel,' Harold said woefully. 'We're the ones to blame. We're the ones who started the decline. We're the ones who introduced rock and roll to the world. Oh me, oh my, what a shambles.'

'But not you, Mister Bishop,' Mrs Mangel said gently. 'You would have put up a good fight.'

'No . . . ah.' Harold shook his head. 'I wish I had. You see, this dancing that they . . . well, it's not dancing, is it?' He smiled reflectively. Behind the spectacles, his eyes were agleam. 'Now give me good old ballroom dancing any day,' he murmured. 'You know, the slow gracefulness of the modern waltz, the cheeky charm of the cha-cha, the excitement of the foxtrot and the sheer devilry of the Canadian two-step . . .' He began to execute a few shuffling steps around the room. 'The breathless artistry of the South American samba . . .' He swung away across the room, then spun back again. 'I was a very good dancer, you know,

Mrs M. Very good. I never had any trouble getting a partner.' He swayed enticingly in front of Mrs Mangel whose own eyes were beginning to gleam.

'Mister Bishop. Mister Bishop.'

'Oh . . .' Harold was still swaying.

'Why don't we put on some old records?'

'A lovely idea, Mrs Mangel.'

Mrs Mangel pointed to the cabinet where she kept her old records. 'Be my guest, Mister Bishop.'

They danced as if on air. They performed a lively quick-step. Harold swept his partner grandly across the floor, they dipped and swung to the syncopated rhythms that filled the room. Mrs Mangel lurched a little unsteadily. She giggled. 'Oh . . . oh, my legs feel like pieces of string.'

The track finished, and another began. This time it was a tango.

'We mustn't stop now,' Harold cried breathlessly. 'The tango . . . so majestic . . . a touch of sunny Spain . . . olé . . .' He snatched a red rose from the vase as he steered his partner past it, and placed it between his teeth.

'Oh . . . I love the tango,' Mrs Mangel cried in rapture.

'Olé. Bellissima. Señorita . . .'

They pranced across the room. They turned. 'Oh, Mister Bishop . . .'

'And dip . . .'

'Not now . . .'

They stumbled. Losing their balance, they fell back onto the couch. They both giggled helplessly. The door opened.

'Nan!' Jane exclaimed.

'Harold!' This was Madge who had just come in behind Jane to invite Harold across for dinner.

Mrs Mangel was still giggling. 'Oh, Jane,' she said weakly, 'you dance with Mister Bishop. I'm quite done in.'

Harold made a wobbly effort to rise from his ungainly position on the couch. 'My pleasure, Miss Harris.'

'I don't want to dance with you,' Jane tersely informed him. 'Nan, what's going on?'

Madge was grimly eyeing the bottles and the glasses on the table. 'They're drunk, Jane. They're absolutely blotto.'

'Drunk?' Mrs Mangel was horrified at the suggestion. 'Mister Bishop, did you here that? She said we're drunk.' She began to giggle again.

Harold had managed to regain his feet, and although he was still swaying rather noticeably, some of his dignity. 'Oh . . . Madge, don't be . . . don't be . . . ridiculous.'

But Madge, after giving them both a look of absolute disgust, had already gone. 'Ridiculous,' Harold repeated. 'What a . . . a ridiculous thing to say.'